The Wolf, The Walnut and The Woodsman

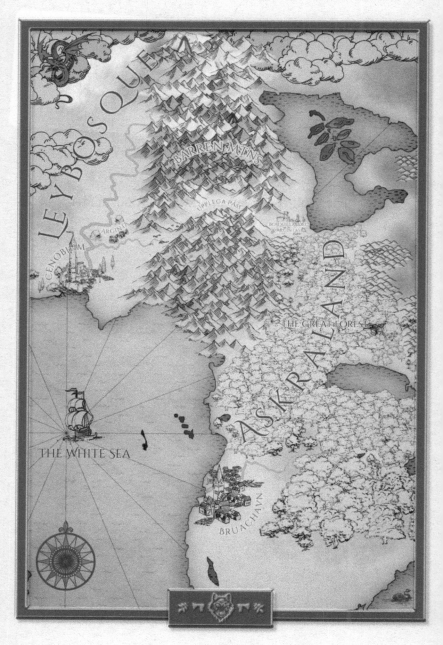

The Wolf, The Walnut and The Woodsman

Gabriel Hemery

WOOD WIDE WORKS

Cover design by Gabriel Hemery.

This edition first published in May 2022.

Wood Wide Works
www.woodwide.works

ISBN ebook: 9781916336247
ISBN paperback: 9781916336254

To the five canine companions who have walked by my side,
To the thousands of walnut trees growing by my hand,
And to my forest of silvan friends,
Especially the fearless, passionate, and the brave.

In the beginning, came light and dark.
Where there was, became lightful;
Where there was not, became darkness.

In the light grew life;
Among life, the living made love,
And love bore power over darkness.
Where love failed, darkness prospered,
Bearing hate, malice, and death.

Those that hold the light shall have power over darkness,
And from their wombs bear seeds of love.
Those that crave the dark shall fear lightness,
And their voids devour love.

ROOTS, I:I-3

GABRIEL HEMERY

CONTENTS

FOREWORD

The subject of this book requires little introduction for most readers, and being a man on borrowed time—as indeed we all find ourselves—I will avoid wasting our remaining moments on fancy and frippery. The tale is so well-known, so widely told, it is surprising how long it has taken for an author to successfully capture, in a succinct manner, the heart of its truth. But then again, it took an author with rare forbearance to risk his own life in bringing this story to light.

If by some miracle you are unaware of our history, you may choose to start first with the epic poem, The Legend of Parousia, which is provided by way of reference for the uninitiated inside the rear binding. If you are a scholar, then I believe you will find much satisfaction from the tale as it is told, with many facts exposed hitherto unknown, all of which are said to have arisen from highly reliable roots. I will leave it to you to debate the facts among your kind.

Finally, a note regarding anonymity. I admire the tenacity of the author in writing under his own name. On my own part, whilst I recognise it may be dissatisfying, I hope the reader will appreciate that merely by commenting on this work I am exposing myself to a disturbance recognised with universal dread.

J.R.

A NOTE FROM THE AUTHOR

You can hold a seed in your hand and wonder how it contains the origins of a life. You may know the species of the seed and even imagine the future plant. But, at that moment, you will not know how animals may effect its form, how the sun and wind will shape it, nor how it will nurture others over time. You will not know its true character, nor its destiny. Only by planting the seed and gifting it to the earth, will that life ever come to be. I give you my seed.

The Wolf, The Walnut and The Woodsman

PROLOGUE

I

Only devils, delinquents, and the desperate venture into the woods in the dead of night, not least in the month of hallows during a howling gale. There was no doubt that the young girl was among the third sort, but at that moment it was the first of these demons that seized Codrina. Seemingly unconcerned for the peril she faced, the girl felt for a missile. Her fingers searched for a weapon of any kind among the litter of damp leathery leaves lying in the crotch of the tree between her naked feet.

Her hunters moved clumsily below, though she couldn't hear them over the flèche of the wind and the parry-riposte of her tree's frantic branches. The forest whistled, moaned, and roared. The three figures approached steadily, spread out in a haphazard search line. A full moon flashed occasionally from behind scudding clouds. She watched their feet stumble across the freshly-fallen twigs and amputated limbs littered across the forest floor, lit giddily by the feeble glow of their swinging lanterns and the pulsing moonlight. The short one passing behind her tree struggled more than the others, limping in obvious discomfort. The man was missing his hat, and his neck glistened darkly, momentarily black as he shuffled through a dancing moonbeam. She waited silently until he passed.

Between the elevated branches of the ancient tree, her little fingers finally closed on a smooth round object. It was foolishly light yet flew from her hand towards the next figure as if sprung from a great yew bow. Passing through the forks of a dozen swaying branches, it fought and won against the swirling currents, flying straight as an arrow. It flew as true as only righteous vengeance deserved.

From her high vantage she watched the curiosity of the walnut's flight. A flash of green trailed in its flightpath, like the most magical of shooting stars. One moment the man was shouting silent directions to his colleagues. Then she watched in awe as the walnut exploded in a sparkle of fireflies as it struck the side of his head. He was several steps behind the others and they didn't notice him go down. The lanterns of his companions faded into the distance, and were soon lost among the shadowed ranks of the trees.

The big man fell like a sack of charcoal, lying motionless with his lamp arm outstretched. His light flickered, releasing a puff of smoke as its flame briefly met the damp leaf mould. Codrina caught a whiff of its comforting scent while she watched him lying motionless in the leaf litter, suddenly aware of the miracle of her ambush. A shiver ran through her when she spotted the dark stained blade of the hunting knife still clasped in his other hand. His face was buried in the leaf mould, yet the silver in his beard was visible and unmistakeable.

The others would be back, retracing their steps at any moment, but if they had noticed and were shouting for their compatriot, Codrina couldn't hear them. She stretched from her crouch, checked that her knife was secure under her belt and readied herself to slide down the slippery bark of the great tree. Suddenly, all her senses told her to freeze. There was an undertone among the cacophony, emerging like a low bass note holding the harmony in a discordant choir. The deep growl hummed under the whistling branches, resonating in Codrina's chest, making the hairs on the back of her neck tingle. Directly below her a thousand leaves swirled into a leaf devil and the form of a great wolf materialised. Its jaws of lobe and petiole closed on the big man's ankle before dragging him silently into the mouldy shadows. A great gust hid the leaf wake left by her foe's lolling head while his other leg buckled hideously.

The young girl was unable to move, not even to finish rising from her position or lift an arm to wipe away her tears. Previously held back by the horror of the night, they now flowed unchecked. Just a moment before, one of her parents' killers had been eager to complete an unfinished task, the next he'd been felled by her own tiny hand, and then taken by the night, or something worse. She began to shake uncontrollably.

2

Earlier that day, as the rising sun urged the forest into life, Codrina had watched her mother at work in their woodside cottage. With one hand she stirred a large porridge pot, and with her other, dipped and folded the family's clothes in a steaming cauldron of soapy water with a pair of giant wooden tongs. Her mother would often say that her dark-haired daughter had limbs like light-starved saplings and should eat more.

Codrina might have helped make the breakfast, only she was nursing the runt of their best mouser's litter. She had named the kitten Aurore after the white butterfly with orange wing tips which filled their little silvan clearing every springtime. She had many chores to come as the 'morrow was market day. The cart was not yet loaded with faggots of hazel for the baker's ovens, split firewood for the big house, or charcoal for the smithy, but at that very moment the day was still hers. Codrina gazed down her nose at the kitten, her deep green eyes full of wonder at the little life she cradled in her arms, her heart content.

Her father was already at work in the coppices, but he

would be home for food by midday. He usually came bearing a wood anemone or bluebell for her mother, and would whirl her round the kitchen in delight at the smell of freshly-baked bread. Her mother would scold him, telling him he was messing her hair or that something was burning on the range, but he'd hold her tightly in a deep embrace until she relented and kissed him.

When she was five years old, her father had given her a quarter-size splitting axe, its light ash handle fashioned by his own hand, its wedge-shaped head made specially for her by their blacksmith neighbour. Preparing kindling for the morning fires and the bread oven had become one of Codrina's main tasks, but it never felt like a chore. She could wield the axe for hours, and would quietly practise her fractions and her aim as she learnt to split a log into halves, quarters, eights, sixteenths, and on a good day, thirty-seconds. After watching her father cleave for many hours, she could perfectly split six foot hazel rods with a billhook, unless the woody stems were old or knotty. Round the back of the cottage, between the rows of beans in the kitchen garden, her father had set up a target made from an oak butt softened in the marsh, and had taught her how to throw her axe. She still needed to use two hands and most of her body to fling it over her head with enough force for it to stick fast, but the days of frustrating practice, as it bounced off its handle or missed altogether, were well behind her. It didn't stop her worrying about Aurore's whereabouts when she practised because if he decided to leap on the target at the wrong moment, she knew she would cut him in half.

Tomorrow wasn't just market day, it was Codrina's eighth birthday. The night before she'd heard her parents whispering together at the kitchen table. Their words were just beyond reach, but she knew they were talking about her surprise, and she was excited because she knew what it was. They had promised her a hunting knife of her very own, and everyone recognised the smith's blades as the best this side of the great river. Her father didn't know that Codrina had spotted him filing the red deer antler for the handle. It may not be a surprise to her, but she'd make sure her parents would believe that it was.

She couldn't wait to go to bed and wake up as an eight-year-old, but first she must shut the chickens away and lash down the covers over the log piles because Father said a storm was coming.

3

I t was a miracle or a life sentence, depending on whose opinion was sought, while people in every generation to come would have a view, even if no one sought it. Whether generating fortune or overcoming misfortune, the events to come created a fable spanning a thousand personal histories, a tale to eclipse any fairy, a fantasy to shatter any myth from ancient times. Some say only the greatest evil was capable of spawning the force for good that was unleashed that night. Others just laugh, more from fear than hope; fear that the story may have been true, fear that the richness of time might still ripen the story, or that the forces of evil which created the legend may yet return during their own lifetimes.

Codrina was preparing for bed and had just stepped into the scullery to complete her last duty for the day when the front door splintered inward. Her mother's anguished scream drove Codrina into the corner of the narrow room and under the nearest cover, and not a moment too soon. Heavy footsteps hurried past, a draft stirring her father's forester jacket which she found herself hiding underneath. A great bellow rang out. It was her father's voice as she's never heard it before, not even when she'd dropped a dozen eggs into a basket of clean washing, or allowed the wolf to take a newborn lamb when she'd left the gate open to the fold. A crash and dull thud followed, and then the briefest rest of silence, before her Mother's screams fractured her childhood.

She could not, dare not, move to look out from her perilous hiding place, not while she could hear the intruders still searching the house. Straining her ears she could tell there were three of them, assuming that her parents were keeping still. Her father's scent filled her senses, and she realised that the shaft of his great felling axe was leaning against her shoulder, propping up his shirt and hiding her tiny form from the evil forces tearing their cottage apart. Ever so slowly, she reached one hand towards it. After sliding the leather guard off its razor-sharp edge, she clasped its smooth shaft tightly in her trembling fingers. Her other hand stumbled on something else hidden under the shirt. Half its length was of hard and flattened leather, the other had the smooth ridges and grain of antler. She tucked her early birthday gift under her belt. Her parents would understand that she'd been really scared.

The violent search came to an end and the assailants gathered in the kitchen. They spoke with words Codrina couldn't understand. She peeped through a crack between the shirt and the wall. The one nearest to her was short and round, and looked like he'd never seen soap and water in his life. Just beyond him a silver-bearded giant of a man ranted at his companion, stabbing the air with a huge hunting knife, flinging blood from its huge blade and his sodden sleeve with every gesticulation. It was only when the giant glanced to the corner of the room furthest from the door that Codrina followed his gaze and noticed a third figure. He was dressed all in black, a hood and scarf shielding his face. Only the glint of the knife blade tucked into his belt separated him from the shadows.

At their centre was the body of Codrina's father. He lay arched backwards, his legs crumpled on one side of the kitchen table, his head lolling over the other. A puddle of blood formed below on the clay floor tiles that she scrubbed every week. It was settling in the little hollow which was always hardest to clean, where a tile had cracked. A thick glistening stream overflowed the puddle like her favourite raspberry syrup, edging towards a second body and her mother's open, yet silent lips.

Aurore came in from the night, tottering through the open front door on uncertain legs, heading towards the scullery and Codrina's hiding place. The men watched in silence as the kitten wove between them and the carnage of the kitchen, mewing feebly with his little tail held upright. With barely a glance downward, the unwashed one stamped his ugly boot down, and laughter filled the kitchen.

Codrina had been paralysed by fear, she had no plan, no idea of what to do or what was to come. Her frozen terror thawed in an instant, and rage led her in full flight into the kitchen, towards the heart of the evil. She swung her father's great axe over her head. It whistled through the air, narrowly missing the crown of the short one. Instead, it took his ear clean off as it sliced down the side of his head. The glancing blow ended with a sharp thud just as her adversary started to howl. He raised a hand to his head before looking down to discover that five of his toes had parted company from his body.

Codrina was making for the front door before any of the three sprang into action. The axe was heavy and she reluctantly dropped it before speeding towards the forest night, hoping that it would take her from the demons.

The forest not only took the little girl, but it consumed Codrina's soul, merging it with its own, preparing her for a new dawn and a life-long quest. And so, the legend was born.

PROLOGUE

BOOK I

GENERATING

WOOD FEEDS FIRE

4

I t was freezing and the child's toes were painfully numb. The boy felt strange in the unfamiliar trousers and waistcoat as he shuffled along in the dark, keeping to the middle of the cobbled street to avoid the open sewers underfoot and the peril of falling night-waters from above. The buildings crowded the night sky, leaning over the narrowing space toward their neighbours, like under-thinned trees in a neglected forest coupe. Silhouetted shop signs creaked on their brackets in the chilly breeze, but otherwise it was eerily silent without the hoot of owls or the rustle of leaves. A brilliant starlit sky twinkled between the dead trees bracing the houses, their timbers framing tightly-closed windows and supporting the ridges of their towering angular gables.

He turned a corner and headed towards the full moon. The bright disc reminded him that against the odds he had survived his first month in the streets of Bruachavn, the capital city of Askraland. As he proceeded, the moon disappeared slowly behind a smoking chimney stack at the end of the street. It belonged to a building which just the thought of, made his stomach rumble. The hot smoke rising rapidly from its tall pots added a shimmer to the sparkle of the stars and confirmed that the baker was making his first batch of the day. As he entered the building's moon shadow the great bell of the cathedral rung out, echoing five times through the narrow streets. Dawn was fast approaching, and he must hurry if he was to spend his windfall safely. The halfpenny weighed heavily in the pocket of his newly acquired waistcoat, and even more heavily in his mind. He'd not stolen before, at least not without making a fair swap, which in his mind didn't really count as thieving.

He still reeked of smoke from his old undergarments, even though his outer layers were freshly laundered. It was an acrid scent harbouring a melding of nasty, cloying smells, quite distinct from a tavern's warm log fire, a smith's charcoal kiln, or an open fire in the coppices. It was a stench that could only have come from an inferno hot enough to set fabric alight, melt cooking pots, and consume centuries-old elm beams thicker than his waist.

The boy barely glanced at the empty bread baskets and the closed shop front, following a now familiar route by turning down a small gap between the bakers and the fromagerie. He pinched his nose at the rancid whiff which turned his stomach, like the streets had done, not so long ago. A four-wheeled cart stacked full of milk churns blocked his way, but he ducked easily under them and scaled the small fence marking the baker's yard. He weaved between neatly-piled stacks of faggots kept dry for the ovens under a large oilskin tarpaulin. The rear door was ajar, and he approached warily in case the wife was nearby.

Five days ago, he'd been unbelievably lucky to receive a half-loaf. It was an act as close to friendship that he'd experienced since arriving in the city. Since then, every attempt at charity by the baker had been cruelly interrupted by his rolling pin-wielding wife. The only fortune was the size of her waist which meant she had no hope of catching the 'dirty begging urchin'.

He hesitated as the warm aroma wafted over him. A memory rushed into his head of Mother baking breakfast bread for Father before he came in from checking the pens. He wiped a tear with the back of his hand and felt again for the coin in his pocket. He absentmindedly polished it on his waistcoat before clasping it tightly in his freezing fingers. He knocked as loudly as he could, until his knuckles hurt, and the coin dug into his fingers. Unconsciously, the boy raised himself on his tiptoes, muscles tensed and senses tingling.

The boy trembled like the nervous young stags he used to watch, nearing their prime, invincible yet vulnerable, proud yet fearful. The type of animal that when hunted would flinch just from the sound of a release and be gone before your arrow struck the tree behind it with the hollow thud of failure.

5

The Eagle and Child was a magnificent tavern, at least it was if the number of its customers was anything to go by. The building dominated the main square just a stone's throw away from the cathedral. Its three jettied storeys and facade of intricate fachwerk, laced with leaded windows, leant out over the market stalls which it sheltered during the day. At night it covered whispering malingerers and bawdy singers until the watch moved them on. The landlord and his family were also high-standing, and no one questioned that this was the venue of choice for the eagerly anticipated regional Wuka tournament.

There was talk of a Grand Master in the city, but nobody believed the tales about him winning against the Smith while playing as the Sailor. As for the whispers of him actually being a woman; these were mostly dismissed out of hand. Those close to the landlord knew that the mysterious character had taken a lodging on the top floor and was most particular in their tastes. Food was to be left on a tray at the top of the stairs and never to vary from a crust of fresh bread, a half-flagon of ale, and a vegetable soup free of meat. The vegetarian diet was cause enough for idle chat, whilst the demand for a fresh walnut leaf to wrap the butter on the side was simply considered an oddity. The room had been booked and arrangements made via a third party who few people could even describe, which only fuelled the gossip blazing at the tables that night.

'I tell you, it is a woman,' said a malty female voice sitting at the head of the table, 'and I should know being the only one among you who earns a coin here. And I'll ask you all this, have you ever known a man go without meat for more than a day?'

'I've traded with the Leybosques who are said to never take meat,' said a gruff voice in reply.

'I've heard,' said a third, 'that those people have tribes made up only of women and—'

'Like he said,' shouted another, 'they don't take any meat!'

Laughter erupted, tankards banged on the table, and several pairs of boots below the bench danced in evident mirth.

'Well, I was on duty last evening,' said the malty female, this time sounding aggrieved. 'You learn a lot about the funny ways of people working in a place like this, and I tell you, it is a woman. Put it this way if you will. I've never found a man whose scent reaches beyond his room, well not a scent like that anyways!'

More laughter, the rhythmic clank of tankards, then a

curse before a trickle of ale appeared between the hurriedly spreading legs of a stocky man seated at the centre.

The voice of the malty female rose to the surface again. 'I don't know you from Eve, but unless my eyes deceive me stranger, you're of the fairer sex. As a woman, you will know what I mean.'

The table fell silent. At its far end a pair of small feet, evidently belonging to the focus of the malty woman's attention, twisted in a circular motion. The toes were delicate as though they had little need of walking any distance or bearing any weight. Underneath delicate sandal straps, the woman's toenails were painted sage green. It was an alien fashion, as was the decoration of both ankles with elegant silver chains.

'Well,' said the gruff voice from the centre of the table, 'what does the stranger from out of town have to say on this matter?'

Silence, this time spreading to nearby tables.

The legs above the green toes moved to uncross themselves, until both feet were planted firmly on the sawdust spread liberally across the flagstones. A delicately fingered hand appeared below the table and slowly raised the green silks of her skirt. Laced tightly against the woman's otherwise bare thigh was a stiletto hidden in a leather sheath.

'Have you no view at all?' continued the stranger's inquisitor. 'Come now, I think it only fair that a stranger sharing a table with regular folk should air their opinion when called upon.'

Now the whole tavern fell silent.

From her hiding place, underneath a wooden bench built into an alcove by the fire, Codrina held her breath. Her back was pressed tightly against the warm stones of the fireplace. She had crept into the back room of the tavern to escape the cold some hours before the main drinking hour began and been relieved to discover the perfect hiding place. One of the dogs had nearly given her away, but when she'd stroked its growling muzzle with rare tenderness, it had instantly curled up next to her, providing warmth and protection. When the serving of food and drink began in earnest, a steady supply of scraps fell to the floor. Brushing off a layer of ale-soaked sawdust was worth the effort when the reward was a lazily cleaned knuckle bone or a fresh crust of bread. The dog enjoyed crunching the bones of their shared scraps.

Codrina noticed that the nails of the delicate fingers reaching for the silver handle of the stiletto were also painted in sage green, and each finger was decorated with a silver ring. The slender blade was slipped silently from its sheath and the silver handle disappeared within the tight grip of a practised fighting hand.

'If I were a girl child begging for scraps, you are the sort who would beat me or worse, rather than offer your help, that I do know,' replied the mystery woman.

'What do you mean by that? How dare you!' roared the gruff voice belonging to the beer-splattered legs which suddenly came to life, shuffling clumsily in an attempt to stand. What right have you to—?'

'I'm a customer here, same as you,' sang the same calm voice, even as the table rocked alarmingly. A chorus of shouts erupted as fellow drinkers lurched for their teetering flagons and tumbling plates of food. The dog whimpered and bolted away from the girl.

The mystery woman's voice sounded like a woodlark, harmonic and two-toned, rising and falling with a mesmerising lilt. When its owner spoke again, it cut through the cacophony with ease. 'Do you think that a woman has not the capacity to win at Wuka or best you in a fight?'

'Ha! Now I know you're crazy, woman. I'm sorry I ever wasted my breath on you!'

'Yet you shared your fetor oris with everyone round this table though, did you not?'

A great roar escaped the insulted man and, as he lunged towards the woman, the substantial elm table tipped over. Abruptly, Codrina's world went dark as the table's toppled surface created a wooden wall to the bench seat hiding her. She hurriedly felt for any food that may have fallen her way. The fingers of one hand fell upon what felt like a well-proportioned ham shank, her others found something cold and sticky. She recognised the wonderful taste of honey-roasted walnut pickle as she licked her fingers. Meanwhile, the now muffled shouts in the tavern reached a crescendo.

The girl was relieved that she was safe from the violence as she tucked into her banquet of scraps, yet it wasn't long before the grunts from blows given and received faded and were replaced by a different timbre altogether. A scream cut through the noise, and then another, followed by stools scraping over floor boards; some kind of shared reaction against a common terror.

Eventually, as shouts of 'fire, fire!' rang out, Codrina realised customers were stampeding towards the door. A rising panic gripped her and using both legs with her back pressed against the wall, she pushed against the table with all her might. Nothing gave; not even a millinch.

Later, Codrina would try to recall how long she waited, listening to an eerie absence of voices and the backdrop of cracking and popping as the heat of the fire increased. When was it that she heard heavy footsteps enter the room; one pair fast and urgent, the other shuffling slow and uneven? The first set started to pace to and fro. She thought to shout out, but something checked her. She sensed a danger greater than the fire. She peeped through a gap between the tabletop and the bench. The pacing feet were out of sight, but almost directly in front of her, pointing her way, was an odd pair of boots with the tip of a walking stick to their side. The toe of one of the leather boots was missing and the exposed part was wrapped in a ball of filthy stained rags. In a trice, she recognised the damaged boot of a kitten killer and fear spread through her.

Suddenly, a pair of sandals with green painted toes appeared behind the leather boots. A woman's voice, like sunlight filtering between spring leaves, filled the burning room. Codrina couldn't catch the words fully, and what she did hear made no sense, '... girl ... shun ... void,' before they were lost to the roar of a fearsome wind. Abruptly, the delicate feet lifted upwards and disappeared, and in their place appeared a filthy pair of black leather boots which shuffled rapidly left and right, seemingly not knowing which way to turn.

The hairs along Codrina's forearms prickled. Without warning, a massive ceiling beam crashed onto the spot where the figures were quarrelling, and a fire ball of red sparks and black smoke enveloped the room.

Codrina buried her face in her hands, protecting her eyes. In the choking blackness she realised her full predicament. These were the same brigands that had killed her parents, but why had they pursued her, and who was the figure that turned her insides out and made her skin crawl? Not only was she still being hunted, but now she was trapped. The table had already been too heavy to budge and now she was wedged in by a giant flaring beam. Even if she remained undiscovered, she was destined to die the worst of all deaths; trapped and burnt alive.

6

Father had told her that it was the smoke that killed most people in a fire. They'd been smoking the bees out of an old walnut tree and she remembered the conversation well. She'd asked why they were using a wet rag to block the holes and he'd explained that wet cloth held smoke better than when dry.

Codrina realised, what worked well for keeping in, would work equally well for keeping out. With difficulty in the confines of her makeshift coffin, Codrina stripped off her ale-soaked dress and stuffed it into the hole between the bench above and fallen tabletop. For the small holes, through which she could still see the bright orange flames consuming the tavern, she scooped up handfuls of sodden sawdust and crammed it tightly into the gaps. As she worked carefully along with her fingers, she found a coin among the filth of the floor, and against common sense sucked it clean and polished it on her undergarments before tucking it into her rolled waist band, next to her precious knife.

She must have succeeded in her efforts because it

became so dark Codrina could no longer see her fingers before her eyes. At least she wouldn't die a pauper. When someone found her body, they'd discover a coin on her body which might just pay for a decent burial. This was Codrina's last conscious thought before she eventually drifted off to sleep.

The slow rhythmic plod of the oxen beat her retreat from everything precious, from everything and everybody she knew and loved. They had been on the road for two days, heading towards the great city, and now they had reached the great marshlands, she knew they must be close to Bruachavn. The little wooded hills steeped in familiar birdsong had given way to long straight tracks raised above whispering reeds. The barley straw piled above her rustled and crackled, scratching her face, and making her arms raw. She couldn't stem her tears and now lay in a puddle of her own making. Every time they hit a hole in the road it jarred her teeth and the cart creaked alarmingly. The cart stopped and instantly she was afraid of being discovered. She moved a hand to the knife in her belt. Someone or something was rustling in the straw near her head. It was a large brown rat. No, there were dozens of them, digging and pulling on her hair, tearing at her scalp.

Codrina came to, whimpering in fright and pain. It was a relief of sorts that she'd been dreaming of her recent past, but in a flash, reality returned. One of her arms was numb and as the blood flow returned, the terrible sensation of ants crawling under the skin of her forearm made her gasp as the tingles marched towards her fingertips. She could see daylight beyond the gap where she'd stuffed her dress. With her good arm she felt the top of her head and was shocked to discover that most of her hair had been singed so severely that most of hair had gone. Her scalp was so tender she couldn't bear to touch it, even with the lightest touch of her fingertips.

She was still trapped in her makeshift coffin. She considered trying to budge the tabletop again, but realised she could hear voices nearby. Codrina lay motionless, catching glimpses of several people raking through the ash and still-smoking debris. There was little conversation between them, just the occasional comment when something notable was found, among them a fancy shoe buckle and a few coins. The nearest figure stepped over a charred object which Codrina's eyes slowly took in. It was a toeless leather boot, pointing in a discomforting angle away from its companion. Shattered sticks of white bone and charred flesh emerged from the boot before disappearing under the weight of the smouldering beam.

The dead figure gave her a sudden chill. Not because of its gruesome appearance, but the realisation and relief that another of those who had hunted her in the forest had perished. Her mind reeled, a hundred painful thoughts and terrifying memories flooding in, reminding of the miracle of her survival and her current predicament. Her damp clothes had probably saved her life, along with the thick elm tabletop. She started to shiver uncontrollably and pressed her back against the warm stones of the wall.

There had been three men who had come for her in the night, and now there was only one. He had been their leader, hanging back in the shadows, issuing silent orders. There was only a single pair of boots lying under the beam, which meant the leader was still alive. Her instinct told her that the mystery figure would not give up his search for her, nor his hell-bent attempts to snuff out her inner flame. If only she could understand why, and how she could protect herself. Perhaps she could find again the strength and force that had come to her during the fateful night in the forest. She had never felt anything like it before, nor since. It was though something from deep inside had emerged from her body. Maybe the spirits of the forest had come to her aid, the trees ... or birds ... fungi ...

Thick black smoke rose and lingered in the room, meeting a grey drizzle of falling wood ash. Black and grey swirled before her eyes, in places dancing rapidly round in dizzy patterns, in others pouring slowly over one another. Something was there, moving behind the smoke, in the smoke, made of smoke. An eyelid opened and a golden eye stared back at her, 'Codrina, Codrina!' called a deep soothing voice.

When Codrina gained consciousness again, darkness surrounded her. She was freezing cold, and her body ached terribly. It was a relief to find that she no longer threatened by smoke. The dream had left her with the strange but wonderful sensation that she wasn't alone.

After listening carefully to check if she was alone, she realised the dark offered her a last chance to attempt an escape. She pressed with all her might against the tabletop, but the great beam which pinned her former hunter to the floor, also kept her imprisoned. Her situation was hopeless. In desperation she screamed in anger, flailing her legs and hitting out at her makeshift coffin. Suddenly, the bench seat above her shattered into tiny slithers of charcoaled wood. She gasped as the cool night rushed in.

She wasn't even sure if she could stand, but she knocked away more of the bench and managed to sit up. The Eagle and Child was reduced to a smouldering pile. Here and there, wisps of smoke reflected the bright moonlight, and a sparkling ceiling of stars arched overhead. With difficulty Codrina slithered out of her makeshift coffin and took a few uneasy steps. A thick layer of grey ash was still warm under her feet. She turned round to look at her hiding place and stared in disbelief. The big table and alcove were among the few recognisable items among the remains of the once-famous tavern. She couldn't avoid looking at the man's legs pinned under the beam, but quickly wished she'd not looked at the body which emerged from the other side, especially the agony of its shrunken face. It was nothing compared to what he had done to Aurore. The kitten-killing coward definitely had it coming.

Codrina hurried away as best she could, crossing the street to reach the moon shadows of the buildings on the opposite side. It wasn't safe for an eight-year-old girl to be out alone in the city after dark, and certainly beyond foolish while wearing only tattered undergarments. She kept moving along the cold cobbles until she reached a narrow alleyway leading away into darker shadows. The buildings parted to reveal rows of backyards, separated by low wooden fences. She stole into the first only to entice a dog into a defensive rage. She hurried on, looking left and right in vain hope, until finally her luck changed. In one narrow backyard she came across a long washing line complete with clothes of all sizes, evidently belonging to a large family. There were three dresses, and while one was too small, the others were way too large. She could hear the dog still barking in the distance, and the voice of its owner shouting for it to keep silence.

Right in front of her hung a complete set of boy's clothes, short only of a cap, and they looked to be her size. She put her hand to her head only to be reminded that her long dark locks were no more. At that moment a new idea dawned in Codrina's mind. No one would be looking for a boy with short hair, dressed in worker's clothes. She hurriedly pulled on the breeches and stockings, a not-half decent shirt that had been fresh darned, and a dark waistcoat with all its buttons. She felt a little guilty, yet silently thanked the unwitting donor.

Smiling to herself, Codrina crept away in search of a

cap and shoes, but otherwise her metamorphosis was complete.

7

Codrina readjusted the coin in her fingers and was about knock a second time on the rear door to the bakery when the baker came bustling round the corner. In his wake billowed a cloud of flour. 'It's just that damn stray dog again my dear, I'll deal with it!' he bellowed over his shoulder, wiping his huge hands on his apron. He winked at the small boy urchin with bright green eyes who stood trembling before him. From behind his back the baker revealed a small parcel wrapped in waxed paper.

How could he have known? wondered Codrina, removing the cap from her head out of respect before remembering the coin in her hand. She stretched an arm out towards the towering figure and opened her filthy hand. She almost fled when the giant before her chuckled heartily, but the smile which creased his eyes encouraged her to stay.

'No, my boy, you need not pay,' said the baker, shaking his bald head so vigorously that his beard wafted from side to side. 'I recognise a worthy cause when I see it, even through my flour-laden eyes. You may have this for no coin, if you promise to return here tomorrow at the same time.

If you prove useful then I will not only give you another pie, but it will be me who'll be handing you a coin. Would you like that my boy?'

Codrina was so taken aback her voice failed her. She stood staring and only realised her mouth was gaping when the fingers of a podgy hand reached out and raised her jaw. She flinched instantly and took a step back.

'Hey, I'm sorry, I didn't mean to scare you, my little stag.' The baker studied his fingers as though noticing their floury state for the first time.

Codrina stood still, unsure of what was happening, wondering if it was a trap.

'If it's the missus you're worried about, don't mind about her. She may look like a deer hound, but her bark's worse than her bite. I can win her round by tomorrow.'

The baker held the pie out towards her again. 'What's your name?'

Codrina noticed the spreading translucent patches in the wrapping made by the still-warm fat. The unmistakeable undulations of a thick crust were visible beneath. Her mouth watered. She hadn't thought about a needing a new name but it came to her in a flash.

She swallowed and answered in barely a whisper, 'Codrin, Sir.' It sounded foreign yet comforting.

The Baker waved her hand away. Words failed her and she nodded hastily, thrusting the precious coin back into its safe place. She reached out to receive the best meal she would eat after four miserable weeks.

FIRE CREATES EARTH

8

Komorebi hurried along the street, her head down with the hood of her heavy green cloak pulled over her eyes against the driving snow. She couldn't shake the feeling she was being followed, and twice already she'd darted down an alley and doubled back on herself. She had also started her journey in a direction at odds to her intended destination. Some might say that such measures were a little extreme and even paranoid, but then such people did not know her name, nor her business. If it had been autumn they might recognise the woman from her painted green nails, but right now both her hands and feet were clad in fur-lined leather. If they'd been observant, they would have been surprised she left no footsteps in her wake, even as she stepped across the thin covering of snow icing the cobbles.

Her mind wasn't fully on the subterfuge, but then it was second nature and she found her mind drifting back to the fateful evening at The Eagle and Child tavern, now three months past. She had been so close, she could have reached out and touched the girl, but then she would have placed them both in mortal danger. Her sixth sense had been right as always, while the fight she'd picked, and the resulting firestorm had been a successful lure. The agony of the distraught landlord and terrified customers had been enough to tempt darkness itself, but she had not expected the diavol to have a willing doomserf by his side, even if he had been a half-cripple. She had underestimated him, and it had almost been a fateful mistake; she couldn't afford to be so careless again.

Tall tales were running rife in the taverns. Traders working in the forest provinces across Askraland had begun to return to the relative safety of Bruachavn's streets for the winter months. Gradually, the tales gained currency and clarity. Stories of many slaughtered families reached the ears of the crown, and several mounted brigades were despatched to patrol the region. Official reports returning with the troops soon confirmed the stories with horrific facts. Families living in the forests were being targeted by a brutal gang of brigands and in every case, each murdered group had included a young girl. The girls' bodies were always mutilated beyond recognition, their eyes plucked from their soft faces, a wooden stake driven through their hearts.

She'd heard the fantastical story that emerged later— everybody had—as it had become the main currency of troubadours in every tavern across the city. Separating fact from fiction was problematic as Bruachavn was blessed with the best storytellers this side of the fearsome White Sea. Certain elements were surely fiction, including versions she'd heard, featuring a great wolf. Every citizen with even a basic grasp of history knew that the last wolf died 460 years ago; a fact celebrated every year on the Feast of Zetsumetsu. Some even talked quietly of the legend of parousia. All versions shared the common facts that a young girl had prevailed against a terrible ordeal with the brigands, overcoming two infamous doomserfs, and survived a visitation of the diavol himself, Xuan.

Komorebi had been on the terrible scene not long after, but of course had not shared her knowledge, as it would put her in mortal danger. When she discovered the forest scene at dawn, the vestiges of the storm were still evident. A scent of geosmin hung in the lazy breeze, while the aftermath of the battle between trees and wind littered the forest floor. If it hadn't been for the storm, she would have known what was about to happen and been able to intervene. Xuan and his doomserfs almost led her to the girl in time to protect her, but the storm he'd conjured as they had drawn close had been a clever foil. She had been distracted by the wholesale destruction of the forest. Yet his followers had not escaped injury, judging by the blood trail she'd followed through the leathery walnut leaves. Then she'd visited the house and discovered the gruesome scene inside, including the bodies of the woodsman and his wife. The girl however was nowhere to be seen. In every previous case the girls' bodies had been wickedly displayed as a sick sign of power. That meant only one thing, one unlikely scenario; the girl she sought had survived.

The snow fell thickly, and Komorebi pulled her cloak more tightly around herself. As the street widened towards the gateway which marked the entrance to the field of the dead near the brow of the hill, it was becoming increasingly difficult to keep a true bearing. The wind had dropped and large snowflakes floated slowly to the ground. Gradually, in the middle distance a shape emerged, its grey silhouette providing a sombre backdrop to the dazzling white descent of discarded angel wings. Komorebi walked briskly towards the ancient walnut tree with renewed vigour.

9

Codrina was settling into her new way of life and at least outwardly, her new adopted family thought the boy was more content. Since offering him a bed to sleep in and two meals a day, colour had appeared in his cheeks and even the occasional smile crossed his lips. He liked to keep his dark locks unfashionably short and wouldn't hear of it that people would say he had the louse. He had been known to speak whole sentences, particularly if his stomach was satisfied and his whistle wetted with a little spicy punch. The boy had been drawn to the visiting fagotter and though unbidden he was always keen to help unload the bundles of dry sticks when they were delivered each week.

Codrina had begun to enjoy her daily routine delivering trays of bread and pastries round the city, and had even drawn praise from the baker's wife for her speed and diligence. In fact, the baker's wife was very generous with her affection. The baker had been right; her bark was very much worse than her bite.

Neither of the two adults knew her true motivation, though she realised that one day she must tell them.

Codrina had come across the smithy the first week of her new self, her transformation still fresh and awkward. Even the feel of trousers on her legs still felt strange. When the shy boy passed the tannery, the other boys attempted to cajole her into climbing the short wooden steps to add her piss to the giant steaming vat like other boys, so she always rushed past. It was still odd wearing a cap, and more than once she'd received a flea in the ear when she forgot to doff to an adult, and she'd had to fight hard to hold back her tears before they gave her away. The waistcoat, however, had been a revelation. It seemed unfair that such a useful garment could not normally be worn by a girl. Its many pockets allowed her to sort the coin she earned as tips for herself from those of the baker's takings. In another was a boiled sweet lifted from the basket of a distracted confiserie stallholder, and in the safest inside pocket, nestled the blue-black striped feather of a jay which reminded her of home, real home that was. Only the hunting knife fashioned by her father and tucked into her waistband next to her skin, was more precious.

Of all the places on her round, the smithy was where Codrina wanted to linger most. Only the fear of displeasing her adopted parents spurned her to move on and complete her round. Her strange interest in its workings had not gone unnoticed. The smith was usually busy at the forge or anvil, but on the occasion of his fourth delivery, when Codrina entered the smithy she found the giant had already put down his hammer. He was slaking his thirst with huge gulps, the water dribbling into his beard before trickling from its braids to soak his grubby neckerchief. On seeing the baker's boy, he sat down and mopped his brow, calling him over. He asked his name and whether he knew something about the workings of a forge. The fine-boned boy had shared his name, but was otherwise mute. 'Don't worry m'lad, I'm not much one for words either,' was all the smith added, and they stared across the yard together at nothing in particular, After a while, both returned to their work.

In the weeks since, the two had fallen into an odd routine. The baker's boy with the startling bright green eyes would arrive with the usual potato, meat and ale pie, placing it near the side of the forge where Codrina knew the smith liked to keep it warm until he took his lunch. The smith would pause in his work if he was able, wiping his hands on his apron before tugging up his trousers in a strangely delicate gesture, before sitting heavily on a log at the edge of the open workshop. The boy would perch on a smaller log opposite and the two would regard each other. If it wasn't snowing or drizzling, they might roll the logs out from under the canopy and sit outside a while to contemplate the weak winter sun.

Things changed the day that Codrina arrived to find the big man cursing. Try as he might the smith was struggling to get the forge hot enough to complete the morning's work. Without a word Codrina had walked over to the charcoal bags and taken a double handful as though weighing them. The smith had noticed the boy's antics and fallen silent, watching in fascination he took a small chunk and sniffed it before placing it in his mouth and chewing on it.

'It's the charcoal, mister,' Codrina said, spitting shards to the ground.

The sound of the words spoken by the boy, and the consequences of the words themselves, almost bowled the smith over.

'What was that you said?'

'The charcoal, it's bad,' the boy added.

'And you'd know something about that would you?'

'Yes, sir. My father was ...' Codrina started, before falling silent.

'Let me see,' said the smith. 'Well I never ... you've put your tongue on it Codrin! This batch is only half-cooked. No wonder I've been having so much trouble.' The smith reached out with a hand as big as a roasting plate and slapped the boy's back heartily.

Codrina staggered forward, tripped over her own feet, and landed face first in an open bag of charcoal.

'Oh, I'm sorry!' said the smith, hurrying over and offering the boy his hand. 'I didn't mean—'

The boy looked up at him. He was black all over, and when his thin lips broke into a smile to reveal his blackened teeth, the smith couldn't help himself. He roared with laughter.

The pair were still chuckling while the smith watched the boy clean himself up with a wet rag. 'What will your parents say when they see you? I think I should explain my side so that you're not to be troubled.'

'They're not my parents,' answered the Codrina quietly, 'but they are very kind to me.'

'Well, I don't mean to pry, but I think I shall come over

myself this Abstinence and have a word. I'm minded to ask if they might mind if you helped me in the forge for part of your day. Would you like that Codrin?'

IO

Rain had come at last and washed the filthy snow sludge from the streets, but it was a cold rain. Under the special cape the baker's boy wore to keep the pies and breads from spoiling, his hands were warm at least. The aroma wafting from its collar cast a magic spell around him, warding off the stench of both the fromagerie and the tanning yard. Codrina had her cap pulled low over her eyes as she made her way down one of the main streets. Unlike other children her age, she couldn't run, not with the heavy tray hung round her neck still half-laden with the remainder of the morning's deliveries. She carved a straight line through the rushing crowd, intent on reaching the smithy with some time to linger. Tomorrow was Abstinence. She was excited and hopeful the baker and his wife would react kindly to the smith's offer.

Codrina took little notice of others on the street, among them a small figure hurrying towards him in the opposite direction, dressed in a green knee-length winter cloak. If there had been a reason to stop and turn around, swinging the heavy tray with her so that the little puddles on the waxed cape spun away, and if she had lifted her face into the driving rain to look the way she'd come, Codrina would have been taken aback. As it was, she hurried on and didn't see the woman stop in her tracks just seven paces behind her and spin on her heals as if a whirlwind had whipped her round. She certainly had no idea she was then followed discretely as she completed her familiar route alongside the cathedral, past the remains of The Eagle and Child tavern where a new building was in the first stages of being raised, and through a maze of narrowing streets and alleyways towards the smithy.

II

Komorebi watched the unlikely pair, sitting next to one another under the covered yard of the forge. They were like a bear and his cub, perched together on two logs matching their stature, while apparently staring at the water pouring in a torrent from a cracked downpipe. There were few words exchanged between them.

She was not well hidden, so dared not linger long. She left the doorway and after a quick final glance at the smithy, hurried to complete the task she'd been set on before the day had taken a twist in such an unexpected yet wonderful direction.

Now she knew where she could find the girl—or perhaps she should now say the boy—she'd be able to able to keep a close watch on ... him. He seemed content, well-fed, and had evidently found somewhere safe to sleep. Komorebi had the feeling that the boy's connection with the smith offered something altogether different from the basics of food and shelter, and it intrigued her. The young child was clearly very resourceful, not just blessed with immense fortune to have escaped not one, but two close calls with Xuan and his followers.

The rain continued to fall in visible sheets across her route and Komorebi could hear the rumble of thunder in the distance. She had cause again to visit the walnut tree and felt nervous to her bones. It was against her nature to visit the same place too often, as habits made an easy target, even for those best prepared.

12

Codrina had tried to hold her breath, imagining that she was trapped underwater, so that she could hear better, but the three adults had now been talking for several minutes after breaking their fast together. With her ear against the kitchen door she'd picked up the odd word from the smith, including that he thought Codrin was a 'good boy' and that he was 'keen to learn the ways...' about something or other. The Baker however was too softly spoken and Codrina could only discern the odd 'ah-uh' or 'mmm' muttered in response to the smith.

'You can come in now, Codrin,' called his adoptive mother eventually. Feigning innocence by taking a few steps back first, she walked loudly back towards the door and knocked softly before entering the warm kitchen. The Baker's wife was seated and her husband stood behind her with his hands on her slumped shoulders. Her eyes were red and she clutched a handkerchief in her podgy fingers. The smith sat at the head of the table with a mug of steaming tea cupped between his giant hands.

'Well, my boy.' It was the smith who spoke first. 'These people have been good to you, and I know that you repay that kindness everyday. It has been decided that you will continue to live here in your adopted home, but work with me at the smithy once you've completed your round. Would that please you?' The big man looked exhausted after stringing together so many words in a single day. He tugged nervously at his unbeaded beard. He combed it out every Abstinence day while away from the heat of the forge.

Codrina smiled inside, thinking it would have been much less effort for the man to have hot-forged the hinges for all the doors and windows of the new The Eagle and Child from raw iron ore. 'If you are sure,' replied Codrina, looking to the baker and his wife.

'We can both see that your heart is not in the making and selling of bread,' replied the baker, 'and it is best for your soul, as well your pocket, that you find a job you enjoy. Mind, you will have to put some muscle on that skeleton of yours!'

It was the best of both worlds, and Codrina blushed with pleasure.

'There you go, it is good to see you happy, my boy,' said the baker. 'You will continue your reading and writing lessons with us by evening candlelight. But enough on these matters now. Go outside and find some friends to play with, it is the Abstinence after all.'

13

Codrina had not wanted to admit that she had no friends to speak of, as she was sure most 8-year-old boys always went round in gangs. Naturally, she knew many children her age, but beyond nodding a welcome she maintained her distance, especially from boys. She helped herself to a small pastie as she hurried past the ovens in the kitchen, stuffing it into her coat pocket. She had a destination already in mind.

While the three adults verbally danced round each other, unsure of what to say to avoid the main subject while the boy was in earshot, they had talked about the cancelled Wuka tournament and other general gossip before turning to the subject of the thunderstorm of the previous night.

Apparently, the ancient tree on the hill had been caught in a spectacular lightning strike, but no-one had seen its flash, even though it happened after dark. Already, there were rumours of mysterious agitations. The tree had stood on the hill for the last 800 years without much misfortune, so foul play must be at hand. After all, it would fit with the troublesome catalogue of misfortunes which had plagued the region over the last year.

Codrina was unsure if her own trauma was included in any such gossip, although she'd heard the troubadours like everyone else. Most nights, images of the doomserfs visited her and brought with them what anyone else would have described as unimaginable terrors. In Codrina's case, hers were vivid memories of true terrors. She would wake with sweat pouring from her body. Often, if she'd cried aloud, the baker would be there standing next to her with a candle, gently shaking her shoulder with his free hand. Recently though, she'd experienced fewer nightmares and wondered why that might be.

Even before she started to climb the hill towards the cemetery, Codrina could see the silhouette of the tree on the skyline. Its skeleton had been cleaved in two as though a giant had wielded his axe from above. As she drew close, she was amazed to find the dark heart of the old tree exposed to the heavens. The girth of each half of the trunk lying on the ground equalled at least a dozen of her waist. Where they met at the tree's hollow stump lay a deep pile of ash, while fragments of the walnut's naked branches lay scattered in a wide circle around the ruined tree.

Others had come to gawk, but miraculously no one yet seemed intent on gaining from the great tree's demise. She'd need to fetch the handcart and some tools from the smithy if she was to gather all that she needed, and move quickly before others plundered in ignorance. She was about to leave for the tools and cart, but something drew her forward. She approached the knee-high stump and placed her hand into the wood ash at the walnut's heart. She perched carefully on its jagged rim and tentatively plunged first one, then all of her fingers into the soft grey ash until they disappeared. Beyond the first centinch or so, which was cool and damp, it became increasingly warm. When her arm was in almost up to her elbow the ash must have matched Codrina's body temperature because suddenly she couldn't feel anything. It was if she had no hand at all. The lack of sensation spooked her, but as she flinched her fingers they brushed against something warm and solid. She drew her hand out and shook the ash free from the object.

As the cloud of fine grey ash dissipated, Codrina gasped. Between her finger and thumb she held a beautiful silver ring. She'd seen one like it before somewhere ... that was it, on the fingers of the woman in green! She bit on it gently to confirm that her eyes weren't deceiving her, before spitting on it and polishing it on a shirt tail. Codrina placed it next to the jay feather in her waistcoat and rested her hand over both the precious items. She could feel her heart beating fast.

Codrina turned back for town, the pastie in her coat pocket forgotten. She was determined to return soon to collect a bucket full of wood ash. She also wanted a clean length of heartwood from the tree. She'd have to hurry while there were still materials to scavenge, and before nightfall came.

14

The anger was too boundless to contain in this world or any another, too voluminous to travel in the roar of thunder, or in the rumble of a mere earthquake. Xuan now knew with certainty that two forces were in play. The hunted child was ignorant, yet seemingly blessed with uncanny luck and fortitude. The ethereal one was sickly pure, fiercely intelligent, but temptingly fragile. He suspected that there may yet be another, but the nature of that one eluded him.

Far below, the dim lanterns of the town flickered in the night. From his vantage, even given the distance between the houses and the field of the dead, he could smell the fear of the townsfolk. It warmed him and his life-force surged.

Xuan stamped on the skull of another of the peasants scattered around the base of the tree. The splintering squelch did nothing to quell his rage, nor did the act of hurling the mutilated bodies one on top of another and crushing them into the fork of the burnt out remains of the tree. His hands pushed through two men and into a third body piled below, closing round its still-warm heart. It belonged to a young woman, but not the one he sought.

Both of his adversaries had been separately at this place, and yet both had escaped. The ethereal one had somehow avoided his darkening bolt, he was sure of that now, and the girl had since visited the same site.

He drained the fluids of the young heart into his mouth and discarded the lifeless vessel atop of the tower of bodies.

Xuan sensed that both his targets were weak. They remained apart and unconnected, but perhaps only by a narrow margin. Had one left a message or a force for the other? What was it that the girl wanted from this tree and why could he not sense her properly? His rage threatened to weaken him further and he was not yet ready to flush out his quarry. He allowed the void to swallow him.

EARTH BEARS METAL

15

Everywhere, the woods lay snow-fast, a brilliant hush smothering every surface, melding falling sky with frozen earth. The pendulous branches of the spruce trees drooped under heavy layers of snow. Only the dark edges of sinuous oak branches fractured the whiteout. Yet something stirred. Beyond the shifting veil of lazy falling flakes, a white unlike the other whites formed slowly before his eyes. It began to take the shape of a tree with two trunks. Gradually, it became clearer. It was larger than the other trees, and one at a time it was able to lift its trunks to walk, and step-by-step, able to begin its steady approach.

She'd been mistaken. The shadow in the centre of the tree canopy wasn't a hollow, but something else altogether. Two pointed ears rose above the tree's top, and the dark patch became its nose. It was some type of animal, streaked white and grey. Impossibly, the sun broke through the saturated winter clouds. No, it was a blinking golden eye! The head turned slowly, and a pair of eyes looked her way, staring into her, touching her soul.

Now that she knew what it was, Codrina was no longer

afraid. The giant animal continued to approach, its deep-furred chest brushing snow from the treetops as it moved towards her. With every step nearer it seemed to shrink until finally it stood next to her, now the size that she imagined any great wolf to be. Its alert ears reached above the girl's waist. Codrina didn't hesitate to slide her hand between them and enjoy the softness of the animal's fur which swallowed her fingers in the softest warmth. The wolf's golden eyes no longer held her but darted around, followed by his swivelling ears, as if he was keeping watch for them both.

'Codrina, I know your true self,' came the words even though his lips did not move, but then he was a wolf, a wolf the girl recognised. 'You may know me as Raunsveig.'

16

Codrina woke sluggishly, as would be expected for any hardworking 12-year-old approaching her teenage years. The dream was a welcome change from the night-terrors, although they were less frequent now than they were when she was eight, when her memories were still raw. She had woken feeling deeply happy and content. The wolf was beautiful and powerful, with a name that matched his character. Raunsveig. He would be a great friend and ally, if ever he existed in the real world. And Raunsveig knew her deepest secret.

It was almost time to rise, although Codrina had a few moments more to herself before another busy day must begin. Her daily round for the baker now took only a fraction over the hour. Compared to the time and effort when she had first started four years ago, she knew every street and alley like the back of her hand, and the delivery tray was no longer a heavy burden. She would spend most of each day at the smithy and now that she was working on her own special project, she needed more time than ever.

She clenched and unclenched her right hand. The tendons in her fingers and forearm ached as they did every morning, although she was getting stronger and could wield a small hammer most of the day. The smith said he'd never seen another 12-year-old manage the furnace and bellows so skilfully, even if the boy needed to build more strength. He recognised that the boy was taller than others his age, but had a narrow frame. When he could afford it, the smith would feed him extra food portions, telling him that an extra pastie or pie would put hairs on his chest.

For a split second, the memories made Codrina smile as she rested in her bed, before her insides churned in panic as worries flooded her mind again. Several weeks past, she'd woken with pain in her chest. It was different to the usual aches which came from working the bellows all day. Running her hands down her front, she had been shocked to discover soft mounds forming beneath her tender nipples. Her chest was no longer as flat as the marshlands. She had known the day would come, but stupidly had hoped that perhaps it never might. After all, stranger things had happened in her life. Her disguise had been so complete, she had successfully hidden in plain view for four years. Now she stood to lose everything and every friend, and would be exposing herself to unfathomable danger. She realised with a horrible sinking feeling in the pit of her stomach, that her days as Codrin might be numbered.

17

Codrina enjoyed a dedicated bench at the smithy, made to suit her height, though she still needed to stand on a low platform to reach the shelves of tools and materials on the back wall. She had her own set of smithing tools which she'd wipe carefully in an oiled rag at the end of every working day before placing each in their allotted place. In the evening, while she tried to concentrate on reading or writing, her mind would often turn to her personal project and to her attempted mastery of the forge. Her adopted mother, who gave Codrina most of her reading lessons, praised her for making such good progress, and by day she often practised by reading posters attached to the walls round the main square.

The smith had told his student to be patient, to learn the secrets of the forge hand-in-hand with gaining mastery of smithing techniques, all the while taking advantage of his increasing strength. Codrina was impatient however, not least because she couldn't shake the feeling she was on borrowed time.

When Codrina described the idea of her special project to the smith, the man had roared in laughter until he realised that his young prodigy was serious. Then the smith had promised his support though he'd admitted such an ambitious article might even stretch his own abilities. He donated the necessary ingot of iron and allowed Codrina to use the forge for the last hour of daylight. Codrina took advantage of this every day without exception. For as long as she could afterwards, she worked by lamplight on the leather and wood elements of her project, until she had to walk home to the bakery.

One morning, Codrina arrived at the smithy after completing her usual duties and found a package tucked behind her oiling cloth at the back her workbench. Once revealed, the bundle stood out like a hammered thumb among the black dust, oil stains, and heavy tools. The bundle was made from a single piece of beautiful green silk and tied with an elegant golden ribbon. It was so out of the ordinary, Codrina felt compelled to hide it under the wool coat she'd worn that morning to keep the spring drizzle from soaking her to the skin as she hurried from the bakery. She daren't look at the mysterious bundle while at the smithy, but it occupied her mind for the entire day. Unusually, she left for home as soon it grew too dark to work at the bench.

Once back home, she hurried through the kitchen with barely a 'hello' to the baker and his wife. She had become so accustomed to the smells of the bakery, she no longer salivated with the scent of freshly-baked meat pies, though her stomach rumbled as she took the stairs two at a time. 'I'll be down in a moment,' she shouted over her shoulder, closing the door to her room and sitting with her back to it in case she was disturbed.

While hurrying home, her mind racing, Codrina realised that she'd only once seen a green silk as fine as the fabric used for the package. It only made her more curious and desperate to find out what it contained. She could picture the green folds clearly in her mind, running like spring water through the delicate fingers of the mysterious woman as she reached for her stiletto, all those years ago, above the filthy floor of the old Eagle and Tavern.

She untied the ribbon and unrolled the silk bundle on the floor between her legs. It revealed three things, all of them surprising her in equal measure. There was a letter, which she turned over and immediately read the opening words 'Dear Codrin ...' No one had ever written her a letter. The writing was beautiful, fine loops of ys and gs arching in perfect harmony with elegant oval vowels, interspersed here and there with intricate capitals. Every line stretched the full width of the page, and the page was full of words, some of them many letters long. There was too much to read in a hurry, but she knew that the words would be important. She hoped she would be able to read them all. Words like these were not created unless they were significant, and besides, they must hold the secrets to the other two items which lay before her on the worn wooden boards of her bedroom.

Three squares of soft hemp fabric were folded neatly and tied together with a twisted milkweed stem. The other item appeared to be a leather cup or tumbler, like those that card players used in the taverns, but oval in shape. In place of a solid base protruded a short spout, so it was more like a funnel. The thick leather was beautifully tanned, and despite its thickness, was quite soft to the touch and surprisingly supple. A single row of perfect stitches held the leather in its unusual shape.

Her boy-name was called from below. The mystery would have to wait. Codrina bundled the items back into the silk and hid the packet under her pillow, except for the letter which she stuffed inside her waistcoat. 'Coming,' she shouted, descending the stairs slowly, her mind spinning.

18

'S ome say that Wuka is the simplest game in the world,' said the smith before pausing to take another swig from his tankard, 'even though it's one you will never truly conquer.' It was strange, Codrina thought, quite how much a good ale loosened the smith's tongue. Not just loosened either, but fine-tuned it, like a troubadour.

'Luck can devour strategy, and knowledge undermine flair, yet there are those who become masters and win every match,' continued the smith with rare eloquence. 'In the history of the game—in the history of all time—there are said to have been only four grand masters, each of whom have conquered playing as either Miner, Sailor, Smith, or Stoker. The fifth character, the Forester, is notoriously difficult to play and there has never been a fifth grand master.' The smith wiped the froth from his moustache with the back of his hand. 'It's rumoured that when a grand master who wins as the Forester comes into the world, the game will be played no more.'

Codrina listened carefully, though the half flagon of ale in her hand was already muddling her mind when she least could afford it. They had finished work early, her master insisting that they went together to celebrate the opening of the restored Eagle and Child. Walking through the new oak-framed doorway had caused a deep shiver to creep up from the base of her spine and up to her shoulders. It had been significant enough for the smith to notice, and he'd asked the boy if he was feeling the cold.

The smith had received a visit from his brother and fellow blacksmith. The two had not seen each other for more than a year, and while walking to the tavern had talked ceaselessly about their work. The conversation continued while they sat together at a table by a large bay window. Codrina was always interested in the art of the forge, but their talk dwelt more on their customers and the politics of Askraland, than on their craft. When the two had mentioned the great game in passing, Codrina had seized on the opportunity to change the subject.

'So, there are five characters,' Codrina asked carefully, willing away the fogginess in her mind, 'and five elements: earth, fire, metal, water and ... wood of course! Why, if all elements are created equal, does one sometimes have more power over another?'

'Naturally,' answered the smith's brother, 'each character has more skill and therefore power with certain elements, like the smith is skilled with metal, fire, and water.'

'But doesn't that mean the smith always wins?'

'If only that were true, lad!' The smith and his brother laughed heartily.

'So how does it work?' asked Codrina, wondering if the

game was fiendishly complicated or whether she was simply more drunk than she realised.

'The heart of the game, its true mystery, is in the four forces which affect the elements. The first one you must learn is the Generating force, where wood feeds fire, fire creates earth, earth bears metal, metal collects water, and water nourishes wood.'

'So they go in a circle, ending up back at wood!' said Codrina, pleased that she'd understood how they interconnected.

'You're right my boy, but it's better to think of them as five points of a star, and that helps with understanding the second force, which is Overcoming.' The brother paused to take another swig. 'That's where every element skips one to overcome the next, so wood stabilises earth, earth directs water, water dampens fire, fire melts metal, and metal chops wood.' With a huge blunt fingertip, the brother drew lines in the grease coating the surface of the table.

'So that creates a five-pointed star,' remarked Codrina. 'Is that how you remember them?'

'That ale's not addled your mind, has it?' laughed the smith, slapping the boy's back so hard he rocked Codrina and the table almost over one another. A tidal wave of frothy ale washed across the greasy diagram.

'He's a smart lad, isn't he?' said the brother, 'no wonder you like to have him around, what with your brains!' The two of them roared with laughter, and Codrina suddenly pictured them as young boys, play-fighting and getting into all sorts of scrapes together.

'It doesn't seem too difficult to understand,' said Codrina.

'Ah, my boy, that's just the beginning,' answered the smith. 'You have worked with me long enough to know what happens when we have too much heat in the forge or too little water to quench a blade. There are two more forces which confuse the Generating and Overcoming forces.'

Codrina took another swig of her ale before she realised what she was doing, instantly regretting the increase in fugginess that would inevitably wash over her.

'So, listen carefully, my boy,' commanded the brother. 'Under the Deficient force, there aren't enough of one thing or another. That's when wood dulls metal, metal de-energises fire, fire evaporates water, water destabilises earth, and earth rots wood. It's like Overcoming, but instead imagine joining up the five points of the star the other way round,' he said, drawing another five lines in the grease.

'And what happens when there is too much of an element?' asked Codrina.

'Ah, yes so that's the Excessive force,' answered the brother. 'It's the same as the Overcoming force, but because there is too much of one element, wood depletes earth, earth obstructs water, water extinguishes fire, fire vaporises metal, and metal over-harvests wood.'

'You see, now they're bad effects rather than good,' added the smith, reading the look of confusion on the boy's face.

'If I get this ... ' Codrina hesitated, 'then every element

can win over another, yet it depends on what forces are at play, and which character is active in the game?'

'Exactly!' both men yelled together and Codrina braced herself for a double backslap, but the brother had already stood up and was heading towards the door unbuttoning his fly, the crowd parting before his imposing figure, clearly keen to avoid an eyeful.

'Why has no one managed to explain Wuka to me so clearly before?' wondered Codrina to no-one in particular.

'It's because you're growing up lad,' roared the smith, before leaning in so close Codrin recoiled from his ale-laden breath, as he whispered conspiratorially, 'it's not a game for the young.'

'Maybe because the forces in my brain weren't connected before now.'

'Sometimes, I wonder where you came from, young man!'

Codrina looked round the tables and drinkers surrounding them, thinking now was not the time to tell the smith any of her story, not that she was sure whether the smith had meant it as a hint or not. The tavern's interior was devoid of character, young and unblemished, its heavy beams unstained by tobacco smoke, its floors unworn from thousands of dirty boots, nor stained by gallons of spoiled ale. Even so, it was packed with people, drinking, eating, and making merry. It wouldn't be long before it regained its former charms. Her eye lingered on the reconstructed alcove near the fireplace ...

Codrina forced her mind to return to the mysteries of the game. 'Can you explain the play, how the counters—?'

Three overfilled flagons crashed onto the table in the hand of the smith's brother, and that was the last thing Codrina remembered before waking in her own bed the next morning with the worst headache she'd ever experienced.

19

Dear Codrin

I believe I'm the only one who knows you for who you really are. You are a true survivor, you are a boy with something extra, a boy with more than meets the eye, yet a boy with a name that is missing something.

Anyway, forgive me for speaking in riddles, but I need you to trust me. You don't know me, but I know you more than you might imagine. I know of your past after tracking you down, I've spent the last four years watching over you from afar, waiting for the moment when we must connect. It is dangerous for me to do so, as you will know more than any other.

We have crossed each other on the street many times, we have even bumped shoulders in the Sunday crowds outside the cathedral. I have passed you pennies for meat pies, slipping extra coin into your purse when you were distracted serving other customers. I have watched you at work at the smithy, followed you to the cemetery, and watched you run past the tannery. You have noticed me only once, and you may know me only for my green painted nails.

She had to pause, to breathe, to rub her eyes in disbelief. The letter writer knew almost as much as she did about herself. She'd been followed and she never even realised! Unless she was reading too much into the letter, this woman even knew her deepest secret, despite addressing it to 'Codrin'. What else did she know and was she acting alone? Did she know why; why any of the events had come to pass?

It is still too dangerous for us to meet in person, except as tumbling leaves in a breeze. I have nearly met my fate twice since watching over you. My greatest fear has always been that if I was able to find you, then another who wishes us both harm might do the same. Our nemesis has become quiet, too absent for my liking, and that only increases my concern for your welfare. And now, now you are changing and we are both more vulnerable. This is why I am writing. I know you cannot ask for help from any other, and you may not even know what questions to ask.

You are growing up, my brave child. Soon your body will undergo major change which will make it harder for you to hide in plain sight. The sarachi cloths are to

*stem your flow of bloods which I believe will soon come
to you. You must expect them every month and always
be prepared. Do not be afraid of the cramps which
come with their passing, it is just your body chasing
away a half-life. Find some dandelion root and dry it,
grind it to a powder and mix it with ginger, then add
hot water and drink it before you retire to bed.*

Codrina knew what this woman was referring to, even if
she was unsure about the word sarachi. A woman's seasons
was not a subject discussed between boys while they
played frogs and pads, or skimmed stones down at the
river, or between men as they talked endlessly of Wuka
tactics or teased the barmaid in the tavern. She hadn't
expected the changes to affect her so soon, but Codrina
realised she knew little of the subject other than
overhearing snippets of whispers between girls.

*As for the other item, this is an invention of mine. One
day it may become popular among every girl and
woman, liberating us from the eyes of men. You are not
the only one who had been working on a special project!
You will know what it is for when I tell you to visit the
tannery tomorrow morning at your leisure.*

Codrina picked up the strange leather cup and turned it
over in her hands, before the penny dropped.

The last thing I must say is that I sense your project is important. Don't stop working all the hours you are given and use the extra time now the days are lengthening. You are right to use the materials you gathered as you intend, including my silver, which I left as a gift to you.

She knows about that too! She must have placed it in the tree ashes deliberately, in the hope Codrina would find it. Who was Komorebi and why did she seem to be acting as his spiritmother? While she had said so many incredible things, she had not provided the answers to Codrina's most important questions.

Codrin snuffed her candle and tried to sleep, but her mind was in turmoil. She tossed and turned most of the night, even imagining at one point that she was in a terrible ocean storm though she had never been on the sea, only heard sailor's tales in the taverns. When she eventually woke, the first light of the day lent a soft pink glow to her little room. She felt as though she'd only just fallen asleep, yet was strangely invigorated.

As she made her way to the smithy, Codrina caught herself taking more notice of others on the street, even looking behind occasionally to see if she was being trailed. She kept a special lookout for a flash of green among the crowds. Though she walked by herself, she was not alone. Someone, a real person was watching over her, not just a creature of her dreams. Someone who knew her true self.

Codrina was excited for another reason. What she was

about to do was so ordinary in one sense, but in another was like being unbound. She turned the corner into a narrow-cobbled lane and strode forward confidently, deliberately sauntering where once her legs had carried her as fast as they could. She'd already practised in the outhouse that morning and had found the device worked well, as long as she clamped it tightly.

She climbed up the well-worn wooden steps, unbuttoned her fly and let her stream play out. She smiled to herself as more steam rose from the stinking vat of the tannery. The sensation was certainly odd, but her spiritmother had been right, it was liberating. 'Well I never ...' said a voice from behind, recognising the frightened child who usually sprinted past the entrance. Codrina buttoned herself up, leaving the leather device tucked inside. She swung round and descended the steps, offering the foreman her hand in greeting, but not after deliberately making a show of wiping her fingers on her trouser leg. The man recoiled in horror, seemingly lost for words. Codrina knew she wouldn't be troubled at the tannery again.

20

C odrina exploited every hour of the lengthening days to work on her project. As the light failed each day, she moved on to her woodwork elements, and now that the messy stages of the leatherwork were complete, she took the parts home to work on after her evening meal. The Baker and his wife always settled either side of the fire to read and knit, but within a few minutes of them relaxing together, their snores would accompany her while she worked, right up until she retired to bed.

The tanner had been surprised one day when Codrina dropped in to purchase a piece of his finest thick hide and some lengths of sinew. They had never exchanged a word before. He even apologised on behalf of his sons for teasing the boy in the past, adding that there was no need for him to add his piss now that he was becoming a man. If only he knew, thought Codrina. Earlier that week her first bloods had come. She could now call herself a young woman, at least she might if she were not in mortal danger.

If it hadn't been for her spiritmother, Codrina could only imagine how quickly every part of her life might have unravelled as her body changed. What would her adopted parents have done when they discovered that she'd been concealing the truth from them all these years? The smith might have been horrified that he'd allowed a girl to work with him in the forge, let alone shared an ale and gossip with her in the tavern. The story would have spread like an inferno throughout Bruachavn, and instantly her life would be plunged into peril. She shuddered at her thoughts, feeling suddenly vulnerable.

'How's it going lad?'

Codrina jumped, her mind reeling.

'You look like you've seen a ghost,' shouted the smith over the roar of the forge. 'You can stop the bellows now, we need but a gentle heat.'

Codrina brought her mind round to focus on the task. This was a critical moment after hundreds of hours of hard toil.

The two of them had worked closely on the project in recent weeks. On the first day of the forging, the smith had stopped his own work to help. Codrina had selected the best charcoal before working the bellows for half an hour to superheat the forge. Once it was blazing hot, they inserted the lump of wrought iron until it turned a bright yellow, verging on orange, before removing it in short bursts while she began to draw the metal out on the anvil. After flattening and peining the rough shape of the form she wanted, Codrina had opened up the back of it into a 'Y' before welding the two prongs back together to form a 'D' hole. They had to return the metal to the fire countless times, bringing it back up to temperature to keep the metal workable. Once Codrina had completed hammering out the shape, they began the tricky task of forge-welding a strip of steel to the blade's cutting edge. This could only be done when the iron was super-hot. Codrina had never seen so many sparks fly and bits of slag fall from a piece as she hammered the two metals together. She was exhausted but pleased with her work by the time they finally quenched the blade to harden it, plunging it into a barrel of cold rainwater. The hiss and cloud of steam enveloped them as if they'd raised a dragon from the earth, which in one sense Codrina thought they had, such was the alchemy of their craft.

Since that day, Codrina had worked the blade for hours upon hours against the coarse wheel of the treadle grinder, and finally the blade of her axe began to look as she'd imagined it. The smith had nodded in critical approval each time when Codrina had taken the blade to show him, turning it over and over, studying the weld of the cutting edge by holding it close to his nose, running his fingers inside the handle shaft, feeling the roundness of the poll. 'You might want to smooth the inside of the shaft, using this file,' or, 'I would lighten it by grinding more from the body here.' And so, Codrina continued to work on its qualities, until finally, the smith had no more wisdom to share. 'It's ready,' he'd said simply, many days later.

Codrina knew about the process of annealing from watching the smith closely over the last four years, and had seen it go wrong only a handful of times. Yet the fact that a piece could fail at all made her nervous after so much effort had gone into her blade. She knew it was a critical process in making the metal hard, yet not to become brittle. When she first started working at the smithy, she'd knocked a knife blade from the bench before it had been tempered and had been shocked when it broke in two when it hit the flagstones.

'For annealing the forge should be like a bread oven, nothing like the heat we used for hardening.'

The boy nodded. Of all people, Codrina should know well the requirements for baking bread, although this stage of forging was quite unlike any baking she'd ever seen. The trick, explained the smith, was to heat the metal and allow it to cool very slowly over several hours. Wood ash made the perfect bed for the metal to lie in, protecting it from sudden cooling. The smith had no reason to suspect that the wood ash Codrina had tipped into the metal box used for the process was anything special. Codrina had saved a bucket load of walnut ash from the stricken lightning tree all those years ago. Komorebi had confirmed what she'd sensed, a feeling from deep inside her body and soul, that this was the right thing to do.

When ready, Codrina drew the hot box out of the forge, scraped out a shallow well, and gently lowered the axe head into its centre with her tongs. It reminded her of plunging her arm into the warm ashes all those years ago, the day that a dozen city folk had been savagely murdered on the hill. She raked more ashes over the top and slid the box back into the gentle heat. Now she would have to patient, waiting until morning to discover if the complex process had worked.

Codrina lay in bed, her mind tripping from memory of work completed, to future tasks, and back again.

She knew the blade would look unlike any axe she'd seen before, except in the dream when it first came to her. She'd seen herself working on the blade in the forge, while the great wolf sat by her workbench with his eyes fixed on her, watching Codrina's every move. Raunsveig's ears were constantly alert to other noises drifting across from the busy streets. It was Raunsveig's watching presence that had given her the idea of adding an image of the wolf to the blade.

The smith had been speechless when Codrina first broached the idea of inlaying the axe head. Once he'd accepted that Codrina was in possession of a silver ring of real quality—believing the boy's story that it had been a gift—the smith had still struggled with the thought of melting down the beautifully-crafted ring. The smith described the process of silver inlaying which sounded highly complex. 'I've never done it myself, but I know the theory,' offered the smith, 'perhaps we should try first with some brass on an old lump of iron.' After hours of experimentation, they had worked out how to punch lines and patterns in the metal, forming an undercut in the lines to hold the softer metal when it was hammered into place.

The inlay work was yet to come. First, she must wait to see if the blade was good enough. Tomorrow she would fit the handle—the handle she'd taken hours shaping with drawknife, rasp, and grit—and she could finally swing the axe into some tough old oak logs to test its metal. The handle measured from her armpit to the tips of her fingers, just like her father had once told her every handcrafted axe should be when tailored to suit its owner. At its base she had formed an elegant fawn's foot swell, gradually tapering the shaft before allowing it to widen again to fit tightly inside the axe head. The smith had been surprised when he noticed the wood that Codrina had chosen. 'Ash would be better,' he'd offered, until the look on Codrina's face made him hold his tongue. He knew by now how fixed the boy could become, once he set his mind to something, and besides he was unsure if the boy would ever swing the axe in anger.

Codrina turned over in bed, pulling the blanket tightly over her shoulders. Her mind drifted back to the day she discovered the ring in the lightning tree. She had picked up a branch of the walnut tree after she'd scooped up a bucket of wood ash. The fact that the branch was already about the right length had given her the idea in the first place. The walnut was thicker than her arm which was perfect as she could cleave it to size, removing the softer sapwood to expose the strong heartwood for the handle. It had dried slowly at the back of her bench ever since and it was a relief it hadn't split or warped over the years. When she'd finished shaping it and showed it to the smith, the man had drawn in his breath as he ran his fingers down the elegant smooth lines of the honey and smoke-coloured shaft. 'She's a beauty, even if she may not be the strongest,' he'd said, failing to resist the temptation to express his view again.

Codrina picked up a scrap of paper and a pencil next to his bed, lying near the protective leather sheath she had completed for the axe head. She had tried to capture the look dozens of times; strong yet gentle, fierce but kind. It wasn't easy, but eventually the face she recognised from her dreams stared back at her from the page. She'd traced the final drawing to create a simpler line drawing which Codrina hoped she would be able to fashion on both sides of the axe blade. She stared at the head of the wolf one last time before snuffing out her candle. She dreamed of Raunsveig through the night.

METAL GATHERS WATER

21

By most accounts the ship was almost ready to sail, but was waiting until morning to depart, when tide and wind would become more favourable. There was also the small yet significant factor that her captain desired another night's stay with his mistress of port, and the two were bedding together in the living quarters crammed over the warehouses. Onboard the three-masted merchant ship, the night watchman was gazing towards the buildings. His mind dwelled on his rotten luck in missing the last carousing night before they put to sea. He also entertained unspeakable thoughts about the captain and his fancy woman, whom he thought was unusually handsome. Suddenly, he spotted an orange glow over the distant rooftops, beyond the tangled silhouettes of the stifflegs and their taught guy lines which crisscrossed the portside.

'Fire! Fire!' No hands responded to his shouted alarm, which was no surprise as there was barely a skeleton crew onboard. There was just sufficient in number to convey the appearance of a guard to dissuade those interested in the vessel or her cargo. The young sailor descended the rigging so rapidly he almost abseiled down, before running to the ship's bell which he rung for a full minute.

The harbour master appeared on the quayside, tucking his nightshirt into his breeches, a lantern swinging in one hand, a cudgel in his other. When the sailor was certain that he'd conveyed the gravity of the news adequately, and instructed a moderately sober crew member to fetch the captain, he climbed back up to the crow's nest for the best vantage.

As the night drew on, and as the glow quickly became a blinding inferno, the sights and sounds of the city ablaze were so terrible they would stay with him for his whole life, not that he knew then how little time was left of it.

22

The peel of muffled bells had woken Codrina in the dead of night, as they had most citizens, as the bellmen from each parish rose to their dreaded task. Through the distorted glass of his bedroom window, she watched the flames leaping above rooftops in the middle distance. The moans and sighs of dying buildings reached her ears as soon as she opened the window, accompanied by the roar and crackle of flames, and the stench of smoke. Nearby, people started to shout, yelling for loved ones to hurry, or with instructions to grab precious possessions. She felt several burning stings on her forehead, alerting her to the wind direction and the realisation that the air was full of sparks and glowing embers.

Codrina dressed hurriedly, pulling on her boots, before tucking her knife into her belt and strapping the axe onto her back. She knocked loudly on the bedroom door of the baker and his wife, making sure that they were awake, and hurried out into the night. As she dashed from the bakery and through its backyard, she heard the frightened cries of her foster mother joining those of their neighbours. It would come to haunt her that she had not shared some final meaningful words with these wonderful, generous people.

As she neared the quarter where the fire had taken hold, she realised that her hunch was right that the smithy was at its heart. The heat was so intense and the air laden with so many burning fragments, she had to retrace her steps and work her way round the side, weaving through the windward streets. Approaching from the rear, she found herself among those trying to fight the blaze. Pitiful amounts of water were being drawn through elm pipes to fill the leaky pails being passed along dozens of lines of volunteer firefighters. Most wore a look of determination and barely spared the boy a glance as he moved between them. Near the ends of the lines stood a huddle of people in fine coats, most holding handkerchiefs to their faces. As Codrina approached she caught a few words. 'Militia ... murdering ... warn ...'

'What's happening?' shouted Codrina over the roar of the flames and clamour of the volunteers. She grabbed the elbow of the nearest gentleman. As the man turned in surprise, Codrina's arm was knocked away by the shaft of a long-handled weapon, wielded by a soldier that she'd failed to spot in the shadows.

'Lend a hand or flee for your life, boy!' came the curt reply from the gentleman as Codrina was shoved away by the pike pole yielded by his moustached guard.

Codrina retreated and made her way along a narrow alleyway, her mind racing. What could the men have been talking about? Was there a greater peril than the fire? Ducking low into a narrow passage it was noticeably cooler, its stones yet to absorb the heat. She was now only a few metyards away from the smithy and as she turned a final corner Codrina was met by an unbearable wall of heat. A body lay near the gated entrance a few paces in front of her, but she was unable to look for long enough to glean any details. The wind shifted suddenly and a cool draft chilled her sweating neck. She lowered the arm she'd used to shield her face from the fierce heat.

The beaded beard was unmistakable, even though his kind face was hideously crushed. The smith was slumped against the wall of the smithy, a heavy hammer in one hand, his other clutched round a wooden shaft which disappeared into his chest. A pool of dark blood spread across the cobblestones, flickering with reflections of the flames raging beyond.

Codrina stifled a cry of anguish at the horrific sight, just as a dark shadow appeared beyond the mutilated body of her friend and mentor. Impossibly, someone was approaching from the direction of the fire itself, picking their way deliberately through the fallen debris. Finally, the figure stepped onto the body of the smith as if it were just another obstacle and a convenient platform. The smith's body curiously flinched under the weight of the dark silhouetted form.

Codrina's axe was too firmly secured to her back, so the girl fumbled for the knife in her belt and thrust it towards the figure with a guttural shout of anger. She'd never threatened anyone with the knife before, but her reaction had been instant, an instinct born from buried memories. She wasn't prepared for the roar of what might have been laughter, and which almost lifted her off her feet. The hot fetid air blasted her face. Half-blinded, Codrina staggered backwards, waving the tiny blade frantically from side to side. She looked again at the contours of the figure, which was so featureless it was as if it had been cut out with tailor's scissors from the dazzling scene. Light from the encroaching flames seemed to find no purchase in its form, and smoke billowed through the ominous profile. It was as though the figure was devoid of substance, sucking life from everything, a shadow among shadows.

'My name is Xuan,' came the words in a firestorm of heat and pain. Codrina doubled over, wincing, trying to keep his blade out in front. 'You are dressed as a boy! I have been searching for a girl.'

Codrina was so taken aback, for a moment she was quite unable to react.

The dark figure stepped down from the body and took another pace towards her, but Codrina stood her ground. It wasn't exactly fear and it certainly wasn't indecision, more a determination to meet her fate. Then events happened so quickly Codrina would for ever have trouble making full sense of them. Impossibly, her friend moved. From street level, a heavy hammer slammed into the figure's black form. An explosion of brilliant light, and yet the blackest of darkness, blinded her. A cry of anguish reached Codrina's ears, followed by a bellowed instruction in a voice she recognised only too well from the smithy.

'Run, Codrin!'

23

In the darkness of the cramped and airless berth, Codrina felt for the axe lying by her side. She ran her rubbed-raw fingertips over the stitching of the soft leather sheath, feeling the coolness of the exposed metal of the axe's rounded poll, before tracing the slender lines of its warm walnut handle. She cradled the axe tightly in both arms, holding it to her chest with the blade lying over her belly button, the handle resting between the mounds of her tightly-bound chest, its smooth fawn foot nestling against her cheek. Tears trickled from her, running over the handle before wetting her head roll. The axe gave her little comfort from the flood of memories which tumbled one after another into her head. She thought of the great kindness and enthusiasm of the smith, of the generosity and love of her adopted parents, of warm pies, and the roaring forge. The ache in the pit of her stomach remained unsoothed.

She was already well-used to the incessant creaking of rope against wood, the smell of tar, and the rush and roar from below, but the roll and yaw still took their toll on her stomach. She much preferred to be out on deck or above, whatever the weather, because it was the only time she began to feel like herself. She wasn't trusted with the ropes yet, and when she wasn't scrubbing the deck boards, she was often aloft. At least she had a head for heights. After all, it was no different than climbing a tree which was second nature for a child raised in a forest, except of course that the three great masts on this ship swayed more than any pine alive.

The first three weeks at sea had passed without much incident. Codrina might have expected some slack as a novice and refugee, but that's not how the captain had seen it. Like the handful of others who were accepted onboard on the fateful night of the fire, she was expected to pay her way. Codrina had been worked so hard, exhaustion had been the only salvation to her sea sickness as it meant she was asleep within moments of going below decks and climbing into her hammock.

Initially they had a fair wind and expected to reach their destination by the next new moon, but they'd soon become becalmed. There was no land in sight, no clouds in the sky, and even the few petrels which came close kept their distance. She couldn't blame the birds, as they were otherwise destined for the captain's table. The monotony was broken only by a brief fight between two of the old deckhands; probably a squabble over a game of Wuka fuelled by plum silvolica. One time, a shoal of flying fish broke the surface near the ship's boat which they'd taken to use for towing them in the doldrums. The four oarsmen had scooped up two whole pails full of the strange fish.

Later the cook had declared them unfit for eating due to the 'thousand darned bones in every one of 'em'. The crew however found their orange roe delicious which they sucked raw straight from their silvery bodies. The carcasses were kept for bait for larger fish as they were already running short of food.

Judging the movement of the ship that morning and the soft slap of the waves, Codrina knew they had another windless day ahead as she readied himself for ship's bell and for her watch to begin. She imagined the final handful of grains passing through the hourglass and the bosun wetting his lips in readiness for his dutiful whistle. She lowered himself slowly, careful not to disturb the old deckhand still snoring in the hammock below, and staggered towards the pail in the corner. The leather funnel was already in place, as was her second nature now, but never a moment passed when her piss flowed and she didn't thank Komorebi.

24

She knew it as the crow's nest, but that made little sense when there were no crows at sea. To Codrina's mind it was an eyrie; a sea eagle's nest in size and in height, like the one that she'd scaled when she was seven years old. It had been at the top of an old pine, just like the nest Codrina found herself in now, and so high she'd felt she was flying. She had looked for their cottage at the edge of the forest, but it remained hidden by a tree-lined ridge. There was a bird's eye view of the shimmering lake where she sometimes fished with her parents, and beyond lay a carpet of oaks which stretched into infinity. She'd watched the white-tailed bird dive to the surface of the lake and grab a salmon. It hardly paused its flight before rising from the lake and turning the fish's head in its huge talons to help fly more easily back to the nest. The clutch of pale eggs by her feet were still warm since she had only recently spooked the male away, and now both parents were mewing anxiously as they circled above.

The bosun's whistle cut through Codrina's consciousness, moments before she felt a tug on her leg. 'Message from below, lad,' came a familiar voice. The grey cap of the sailor, familiar from the lower hammock, surfaced above the rim of the crow's nest before his crooked smile appeared, framed by white whiskers. 'Them with a concern for our souls wonder if you weren't asleep on look out.'

'Sorry, I mean, I was daydreaming that's all,' stuttered Codrina.

'You might think the captain has a soft spot for you after letting you aboard, but you should watch yourself, or the bosun'll have you whipped, whether dreaming the day sort or night sort.'

'I know,' Codrina answered. 'Can you tell him I was thinking?'

'I should be thinking of a better excuse than that lad, before you come back down!' The sailor disappeared from sight, chuckling to himself as he scrambled down the rigging like a pine marten.

Codrina lifted the heavy glass to her eye and studied the horizon carefully at every point of the compass. There was nothing but sea and haze, though she wondered if clouds were beginning to mass to the far west. She decided to say nothing yet, but would keep her eye peeled in that direction.

She wasn't sure why they always had someone posted on lookout. It wasn't as if there were known to be brigands about, or pirates for that matter, not that she was sure she knew the difference.

25

Codrina used every muscle of her lithe body to whirl the axe over her head in a single fluid movement, as elegant as any street dancer on the Feast of Zetsumetsu. The axe not only held up to Codrina's first swing, but cleaved the great lump of hardened bog oak in two, like it was mere kindling.

The smith was still agog when the boy turned on his heals, strode ten paces across the yard and, without pausing, swung again. Codrina loosened her grip on its shaft, making a tiny unconscious adjustment with her finger tips to the accelerating fawns foot, before allowing the finely-crafted axe to fly.

Both of them watched it tumble, head over shaft, slicing through the flakes of the late spring snowfall as if its flight had been commanded to slow by the spirits for their personal delight. When it hit one of the lumps of oak squarely and that too split in half, the big man stood unmoving, rooted to the spot. It was as if the axe had taken his tongue en route, as he gaped first at the log, then at the boy, and back again.

'Well I never ... I never ... ,' stumbled the smith, 'I've never in all my years seen anything like that.'

Then the great man grabbed the boy in a bear hug and almost squeezed the life out of Codrina as he roared with laughter before dancing round the yard with the boy in his arms flapping like a rag-doll.

26

The gentle flapping of canvas woke Codrina. The recollection brought a painful smile to her dry cracked lips. She was surprised that she'd dozed off again and sat up quickly, trying to look alert, yet feeling quite the opposite.

There was definitely a breeze, though the water remained as smooth as a looking glass. She leaned out so she could see below, but there was no one in the rigging who would have spotted her snoozing again, and even the main deck was languorously quiet. Codrina sat up straight and felt the hairs on her neck stir a little as she raised the heavy brass teleglass to look again towards the west. She had wondered whether change was coming, but now there was no doubt about it.

Codrina's report kindled a great deal of activity on the ship, her indiscretion seemingly forgotten, especially after an experienced deckhand had confirmed the same sighting from the crow's nest. Codrina hadn't witnessed the captain raise his voice or look agitated, though he never shied from issuing stern orders. In keeping with his usual manner, he began to impart quiet instructions to small groups of men, before they dispersed purposefully throughout the ship. Some trimmings were made to the canvas above, but otherwise everything was lashed securely or removed below decks.

The bank of distant clouds begun to engulf the setting sun. For countless nights the sun had dipped unblemished below the horizon, signalling another quiet night for the waning moon to take the watch. Tonight, the head of a black serpent appeared to have lunged from the deep, its angry snarl snapping at the red and purple skin of a blood fruit. Rays of yellow and orange sprayed briefly across the darkening azure sky, turning crimson and violet as night loomed. When the first stars began to twinkle in the east, a distant flash of lightening lit up a row of jagged clouds on the spine of the western horizon.

The captain stopped Codrina as she crossed the quarter deck and spoke to her urgently. It was only the second time he'd said anything to Codrina directly, since allowing her to come aboard.

27

Though she was exhausted, Codrina found it difficult to sleep with the mares running through her head. She knew the ship was as storm-ready as it could be and that grabbing a little sleep was the best course of action, especially while the sea remained calm.

When she'd listened to the sailors' tales in the tavern, or to a troubadour's lament, she was forever grateful for the firm flags under her feet and the warm fire by her side. The adventures and misadventures they described were so gripping and otherworldly, but never urged her to sail. But now, now she was on the infamous White Sea herself, about to enter the eye of a storm, a storm about which even the unflappable captain had privately expressed grave concerns.

The inferno that swept her former life away on land, had almost carried her soul into the arms of a demon. It had been truly terrifying, but Codrina was beginning to fear what was to come, even more. A night storm in the White Sea was no place for a child of the forest. She had no idea what had become of Komorebi the night she fled the city, whilst Raunsveig had not visited her dreams since she'd been at sea. All she knew was that the people she loved and who cared for her, were no longer by her side, let alone alive in this cruel world. She was now by herself, and she would survive only through the course of her own actions.

28

Memories of her flight through the streets—visions of the firestorm, gangs of marauding militia, and the mutilated bodies of innocent citizens—dissipated as the ship lurched violently, only to be replaced by a gut-wrenching fear of her current predicament.

The ship shuddered as if suddenly out of tune with the raging rhythm of the storm. Codrina's hammock swung alarmingly first one way, then the other, yet it was the angle of the candle lantern seen against the solid deck beam which brought the captain's words back to her.

'You are young, lad. Let me lend you some wisdom,' he'd said quietly to Codrina on the quarterdeck, his hand resting on her shoulder as if to emphasise the point. He leant in closer still. 'She has never been good in a storm and I fear we are carrying too much iron ore for our own good.'

Codrina had stared blankly at the man for a moment before the words formed some meaning.

'If this storm is severe as it looks, we could be in trouble,' he added. 'Prepare, quietly mind, for the eventuality that we may go down.'

The captain had shared the news in such a matter of fact way, Codrina simply nodded.

'Do you hear me, boy?' he added, squeezing her shoulder firmly.

'Yes, I understand,' answered Codrina finally. 'Why ... I mean, what should I do?'

'Top up your flask with drinking water and tie it together with your worldly possessions to yourself. If the storm truly takes hold of us, stay on deck, preferably keeping near the small boats.'

Codrina almost fell out of her hammock and staggered to the companionway ladder, the listing of the ship and another violent lurch hurrying her forward involuntarily. As she reached the top tread and raised the deck hatch she was instantly soaked to the skin. As she wiped the saltwater from her eyes, the scene unveiled before her was a living nightmare. The ship was noticeably listing, the deck leaning towards the lee of the storm and one after another, heavy waves broke through and over the bulwark. The mizenmast had splintered in two and a tangle of canvas and rope littered the stern. A gobbet of sailors was attempting to cut it free with the aim of releasing the top half which leant out into the darkness.

Codrina moved forward, intending to help with her own axe, but as she made her way aft, lightening fractured the night and the sight stopped her dead. The serpent had finally reached their fragile wooden craft, and a wave several times higher than the crow's nest hung over them, its angry white crest poised to strike above a cavernous wall of water.

Water Nourishes Wood

29

The woman knelt on the damp earth, light drizzle wetting her hood which she had pulled fully over her sensitive scalp to protect it from the needling pain of the cold droplets. Some of her hair had already fallen out, leaving ugly patches of angry blistered skin, in other places clumps of singed and frizzled hair remained, but they were likely to fall out soon. From her vantage on the top of Cemetery Hill, Komorebi gathered her cloak tightly round herself and gazed in horror at the ruined cityscape below.

An ugly black wedge had been carved through the tightly-packed buildings of Bruachavn. At the sharp point of the wedge she knew lay the remains of the smithy, its craft and industry lost forever, the spirit and kindness it had forged, stolen by an act of pure evil. The gigantic wedge of charcoaled buildings fanned out from the smithy towards portside. Only the stonework of the cathedral had protected the building from the intensity of the firestorm, and its pale stone sides looked painfully out of place in the scene of suffering surrounding it on every side.

On her way to the hill, Komorebi had picked her way

between clay pots, tiles, and cooking pots, horribly melted and deformed into unnatural shapes. Her feet followed rivulets of lead solidified between the cobblestones. Many of the bodies waiting to be cleared, remained where they had fallen in agony, their charred remains leaving nothing behind as to their identity. Many of them had crushed skulls and the contents of their boiled brains pooled in grisly black puddles around their crowns. They lay in every street and square, giving the impression that Bruachavn had been descended upon by fallen angels.

A layer of smoke still hung over the entire city, and its cadaverous vapours clung to her cloak. Komorebi raised her face to the rain and breathed in deeply, the cool clean air purging her sore lungs. Then she sobbed. She cried for those lost, she howled for the power evil held over good. She pummelled the earth in frustration for her weakness, and for her failure in protecting the child.

Everyone had lost someone and so many bodies were burnt beyond recognition, no one was interested in another person's loss. A terrible fear gripped Bruachavn, its mourning citizens struggling to understand the nature of the forces which had descended in the night. It was no surprise that her quest for information among the devastated streets had yielded little.

A glimmer of light emerged from the darkness when Komorebi discovered there was no child's body at the smithy. The remains of a large-framed man was the only body she found nearby, and the heavy hammer clutched in his hand removed any doubt that it was the smith. Around him there was no debris of any sort. The walls of the narrow street where he lay had fallen outwards in every direction. He lay at the epicentre of an event of some kind, Komorebi was sure of it. She was also sure that Codrin had probably been at the scene at some point, as the child was too resourceful and mindful of others to have stayed away.

Komorebi held onto another slither of hope. Following the path of the fire had led her eventually to portside which remained mostly undamaged. A roof above the city grain store had collapsed and a mountain of barley smouldered inside, lending a smell of the tavern to the sea air as she made her way towards the harbourmaster's quarters. Once the man had overcome his salty mood after being raised from his bed, even though it was mid-morning, he eventually confirmed that a merchant ship had slipped out in the night. With a fully-laden cargo, which included several barrels of gunpowder, he had urged the ship to put to sea despite the shallow rising tide. With further pressing, the fatigued man confirmed that the ship had taken some refugees on board at the last minute as the captain was short of hands. In the chaos, no names or details had been recorded.

On the hill, Komorebi wiped the tears from her eyes, her gaze moving from portside to where the smithy once stood. There was a slim chance, and that was enough to cling to, with every hope she could muster. She must decide what move to make next. Xuan was increasingly bold and ever more desperate, and time was not on their side.

Komorebi leaned sideway and placed her hand on the stump of a once great tree. All around its perimeter, little green shoots had sprouted from the bark, creating a ring of miniature walnut saplings. Its slight hollow had collected a small pool of water and she leant over it to stare at its surface. A living green halo framed her face as she gazed at her worried reflection.

30

One moment, Codrina was held aloft and kept afloat by the carefully reconstructed skeleton of an ancient forest, the next he was blind in perfect blackness. One moment, her lungs inhaled and exhaled involuntarily in perfect unison with her environment, the next she was unable to breathe. One moment, her ears were attuned to the fury of the storm, helping balance her body against the violent death throes of the ship, the next she was suffocating in silence with no concept of up or down. Unable to transition from one world to the next, unlike a flying fish, Codrina's senses were flooded in an instant.

Codrina had no idea how long it was before her head broke the surface and when she was able finally to gasp desperately for air. Almost immediately, something heavy hit her between the shoulder blades, pushing her below the waves again. As she frantically fought to recover amid the swirling currents and submerged flotsam, her hand brushed against a taught rope. She grasped it desperately and managed to pull herself upwards, back towards the surface. It took all her strength to haul herself out of the waves high enough to get one leg over the raised sides of the floating object, followed by an arm, and eventually the remainder of her exhausted body.

It took Codrina a few moments to realise that she found herself once again in the crow's nest, but this time she was at sea level and half her body was submerged within the shelter of its raised wooden sides. Suddenly, she screamed in pain as her fingers became trapped between the rope and the rim of the nest. There was a pull of increasing strength from below, threatening to drag them under. She fumbled for the knife in her belt and as soon as it was in her hand, she frantically started to cut through the taught rope. The yarns began to split one by one, millinch by millinch, while her little life-raft continue to tilt alarmingly. Finally, with two strands cut, and halfway through the yarns of the third, it snapped free and she fell back into the nest. Her relief was short-lived and fragile.

The storm raged on through the night. One huge wave after another crashed over her frozen huddled body as she clung on desperately to the sides of the nest. Codrina eventually accepted that she and her little craft might just remain afloat and stay upright, however much water washed over them, so she decided to lash herself to it using the remains of the rope she'd cut earlier. It was the longest night of her life, but eventually Codrina drifted into a fitful sleep.

Codrina woke with the reflection of the sun dazzling her eyes from the pool of water around her waist. She couldn't believe that she had survived the storm. The nest rose and slowly spun with the gentle rolling waves, and as she took in her surroundings, the true peril became clear. She and her wooden craft were a lonely miracle in a vast ocean desert. It was if the ship itself had never existed, with no sign of any floating debris expect her own little raft, let alone any fellow survivors. All Codrina had with her were the ragged clothes clinging to her sodden body, attached to her belt hung her flask of drinking water and her knife, and strapped firmly to her back, her precious axe.

Far from being a fish out of water, she was like a woodsman without trees to nurture. Her life had become a falsehood, her true self always out of reach, while her promise to herself and others she loved threatened to remain forever unfulfilled. Why was it, she wondered, that every chapter of her life led ineluctably to the next, generating one ill-fated event after another? She needed to find a way to break the cycle, and if she was very lucky and managed to survive her current predicament, she must discover how to overcome any remaining hurdles.

Little did the child know how, line by line, and chapter by chapter, she was fulfilling the legend of Parousia. Nor could Codrina have known that she was only halfway through her passage rewriting the history of the world.

BOOK II

OVERCOMING

WOOD PARTS EARTH

31

The two Cenobites ambled along the shoreline. Their progress was slower than the younger one wished. Once their patrol was over, Karişkir was expected to help in the kitchen, preparing the evening meal. The thought only made her more impatient as the duty came with obvious perks. Given her time of the season, she was craving sweet foods, and she would be able to surreptitiously satisfy them while Cook was looking the other way. Her patrol companion was the oldest in the community and it was a true miracle that she was able to complete the route at all, given her celebrated age. Yet, while she was slow in body, Krummholz's mind was still the sharpest among them all, as Karişkir was cruelly reminded earlier as they descended the cliff path, painfully slowly. She was chided for forgetting the words of the fourth canticle, which every novice was expected to learn by heart along with the other 11. But then, Karişkir was struggling to focus on anything much, which was unsurprising given that she had scaled the walls after dark and enjoyed an illicit evening with local girls from the nearby town.

They approached their halfway point, marked by the craggy headland which presently hid the Cenobium from view, even though it was perched high on the cliffs overlooking the next bay. Karişkir and Krummholz continued their slow progress, keeping close by the high tide mark while trying to avoid the loose shingle peppering the otherwise sandy shore. The onshore breeze had picked up, finally dissipating the sea fog which had plagued them recently. Since the previous quarter, an unusual quantity of nautical flotsam had washed up, leading to much speculation as to whether a ship may have succumbed to the great storm which had swept through, prior to the new moon.

Karişkir skipped forward to retrieve a pale object washing to and fro in the waves. The pale canvas shoe was much larger than the leather moccasins she wore on her own feet which meant it probably belonged to a male sailor. The community's speculation may have been right after all. It appeared well-worn and Karişkir imagined it working hard to protect its wearer while he scaled the tall masts, fought off pirates, or scrubbed the decks, although she had only ever read the descriptions of a ship in the books of the library.

The 13-year-old shook copious amounts of sand out of the shoe and added it to her backsack. Krummholz must have found a burst of energy, either that or Karişkir had spent longer than she thought dreaming about the shoe and its wearer. When she looked up, the hunched figure of her companion was already disappearing round the point. Karişkir lifted her green habit and made a beeline for the old woman, sprinting through the surf and enjoying the rush of sea air through her hair.

She was breathing heavily when she paused at the point and was surprised by how far ahead Krummholz still appeared, her figure obvious along the smooth sands of their home bay. Thank the stars the old Cenobite had stopped to wait. Karişkir thought Krummholz looked more hunched over than ever, before realising her companion was bent over something large on the edge of the surf. She appeared to be struggling to keep it from floating back out to sea. She sprinted forward again wondering whether it was a part of a ship, perhaps the torso of the shoe's owner. She might even get a glimpse of a man's phallos and orbs.

As Karişkir drew close, her eyes recognised the large object as a round bathtub, like the one they had in the infirmary. Krummholz was now prostrate in the surf, hanging on desperately as the waves washed to and fro. It was only as she drew near that Karişkir realised why the tub was proving so difficult to control. The tub wasn't empty! She couldn't believe her eyes. As she dragged the tub towards the beach with the help of the surging waves, her eyes took in the partially-clothed body it nurtured inside, curled up as tightly as a babe. Its chest was swaddled in tight bandages, yet otherwise the figure was naked below the waist, its slim legs raised enough to reveal a clump of dark curly hairs foresting the origins of human life. Between the woman's sharp shoulder blades, held in place by a breast binding, lay a fearsome-looking axe.

This was so much better than anything that a man could offer. They'd discovered a female warrior from a foreign land and judging by the tiny movements of her skeletal ribs, she was still alive!

Blessed are the believers,   for they will inherit the earth.

32

CANTICLE OF CENOBIUM

Blessed are the believers.
for they will inherit the Earth.

Be strong and be sure,
For you are the future,
And great will be your reward.

Blessed are the seeders,
for they grow our future.
Refrain

Blessed are the forgers,
for they equip us to succeed.
Refrain

Blessed are the miners,
for they light up our lives.
Refrain

Blessed are the stokers,
for they drive us forward.
Refrain

Blessed are the sailors,
for they shrink our world.
Refrain

Blessed are those who pursue darkness
for theirs is the glade of life.

Glory to the Mother and to the Daughter,
And to the silvan spirit,
As it was in the beginning,
And will be for ever more.

Be strong and be sure,
For you are the future,
And great will be your reward.

33

The chanting floated through the cloisters of the infirmary, its high notes ringing from the stone pillars separating each wooden bed. Rays of weak sunshine filtered through open windows, their fabric covers billowing gently in the morning breeze. The infirmarian bustled from bed to bed administering a honey and ginger tea. The challenges of caring for her new charge were considerable and she felt only a little guilt for abstaining from the office of dawn prayers. There was almost always a resident elderly Cenobite who needed her care, and occasionally a sick younger woman with the cramps or a fever. There were also of course the occasional malingerers who were best treated with a spell working in the kitchen garden, yet rarely was an outsider granted any care, let alone candle-long care at that.

The special patient—whispers were she was a warrior—had been with them now for four days and her carer had found little time for sleep since. The poor young woman had yet to regain consciousness, although some of the festering open wounds were beginning to heal under the beeswax poultices she applied each day. The ugly wrinkles in the patient's grey skin had filled out and gained a pinkish bloom. The infirmarian noticed burn scars under her cropped dark hair which only increased the mystery surrounding the woman. Three times a day the infirmarian gently rolled the woman onto her side and squeezed water between her cracked and blistered lips using a cloth wetted with water freshly drawn from the well.

On the small bedside table lay the axe the warrior was found wearing, bound to her body. It was quite unlike any tool they used for their toil in the coppices, and just glancing at it caused a shiver to erupt between the infirmarian's shoulders only for it to trickle wickedly down to her hips. She tried to avert her eyes when she remembered, unlike that mischievous young novice Karişkir, who was fixated with it. Every time the novice visited the infirmary—which seemed to be during every caesura between her normal duties—the infirmarian noted how she handled the fearsome axe. She rested it on her knees among the green folds of her habit while she cradled the patient's hand and whispered her prayers. The warrior's saviour was forming a bond with the mystery woman she had unearthed, which was only to be expected. The infirmarian would have to watch that it remained a healthy fascination.

34

The sea was unusually still and the clouds strangely uniform and bright. A flock of white gulls circled overhead in perfect symmetry, their arched wing tips joining above grey pillars of water rising from ...

Codrina came to with a start, her eyes darting left and right, trying to resolve the strangeness. She was not on the deck of a ship as she had thought, nor even on the sea, but in a stone chamber. Her heart hammered in her chest. A warm hand squeezed her fingers.

'She's awake. Hurry, hurry!' cried a female voice by her side.

Codrina moved to shake her hand free, but she had so little strength her arm barely twitched.

'Don't move, please don't worry,' came the voice again, this time whispered calmly, close by her ear. 'You're quite safe.'

The woman's breath smelled of mint and cloves. A wisp of red hair, straying from the headdress which otherwise covered the woman's head, brushed against Codrina's face. Behind her the sound of hurrying footsteps echoed across the stone chamber.

Codrina managed to turn her head. In front of her sat a girl, perhaps with the same number of years. Their eyes met briefly, before the girl glanced quickly over her shoulder towards the approaching figure.

'My child, my dear child,' started the perfectly round woman, dressed head to toe in green, including the headdress which framed her rosy face. 'You are back with us, thank the merciful spirits.'

'We found you, down by the sea in—' started the young one.

'Hush Karişkir, now is not the time.'

Codrina looked from one to the other, taking in their strange matching clothes, trying to decipher the look that passed between them. She opened her mouth to speak but only a rasp emerged.

'Quickly, fetch the girl a beaker of fresh water,' instructed the older woman.

Footsteps skipped lightly across the chamber. Codrina licked her lips. They were swollen and painful. Something else troubled her mind ... The woman had said 'girl'. They knew her as a girl. She focussed on her own body, sensing with relief that though she was weak, she could feel both her legs and arms. She was definitely naked underneath the sheet. Her mind reeled.

'Here you are, sister,' said the younger one. 'I'll bring it to your lips. Careful now, take small sips.'

Water had never tasted so good. Its progress inside her body was invigorating, beyond anything she'd ever imagined.

'Are you really a warrior?'

'Karişkir, enough!' scolded the older woman.

Codrina followed the glance of the younger one as her eyes flicked towards the table beside the bed. It couldn't be ... it was! Her axe was there, lying within easy reach, if only she could move. Whoever these people were, she was at their mercy, but if they had wished her harm she wouldn't be lying before them alive, feeling the cool water settle inside her feeble body.

35

Codrina found herself wondering if this is what it was like to have a real friend, at least a friend of similar age. She'd only ever trusted adults before, and animal kind of course, so it had taken her by surprise when she began to look forward eagerly to Karişkir's next visit to her bedside. Over the previous seven days, ever since she had regained consciousness, she had been told a multitude of amazing things in whispers, giggles, and proud tales; all of it surprising, some of it eye-opening, while a few insights shook her to her core. Early on, she had also come to a momentous realisation by herself, even before she found the strength to speak.

Mother Elder had come to her bedside the evening of her recovery, flanked on one side by Karişkir, and on the other by the infirmarian. From behind the assembly of sisters shuffled the oldest woman she had ever laid eyes upon, introduced as Krummholz, who despite her age seemed as sharp as a needle. Karişkir explained that it was the elderly sister who had first come upon Codrina in the surf and, somewhat unbelievably Codrina thought, prevented her from being washed back out to sea. Codrina wandered what it must be like to have such a deformed spine, but smiled and nodded weakly in gratitude. The woman had painted a strange symbol in the air between them before smiling with sufficient vigour to expose her toothless gums. But there was something else that fought for Codrina's attention all the while Mother Elder progressed through her introductions of one sister after another.

When Mother Elder had eventually perched on the side of the bed and taken one of Codrina's hands in her own, the girl glanced down and was unable to prevent a little gasp from escaping her lips. The Mother's head tilted in surprise as she followed Codrina's gaze inquisitively. Every one of the woman's long slender fingers bore a silver ring, and her nails were painted green, matching the habits worn by the sisters. The Mother took a breath, poised to say something as she studied the girl before her carefully, before reconsidering and pursing her lips. Slowly, her eyes never leaving Codrina's, she let go of her hand and rose with the bearing of a natural leader.

'Sisters,' she started, her words ringing through the cloisters as she smoothed the front of her habit with her hands, 'we thank the spirits for the safe revival of this young woman, and the lifesaving skills bestowed upon our infirmarian.'

'In truth,' came a reply in unison, while more figures were scribed in the air by a number of the sisters.

Mother Elder spared a final glance at Codrina before leaving with a wash of sisters in her wake.

Codrina's new friend lingered, and approached the bed. 'Karişkir, you are expected soon for vespers,' came the voice of the infirmarian from beyond the arched entrance.

Karişkir continued forward, settling herself in the warm depression left by her superior. 'Her name is Ki,' she said finally, 'but we call her Mother Elder.'

Codrina nodded, but by then her mind was spinning.

36

Thanks to Karişkir, Codrina gained a great deal of information about the workings of the Cenobium, the nature of the sea and forests surrounding the spiritual fortress, and the country of Leybosque itself. Contrary to tavern tales back home, the Leybosques were not a people consisting entirely of women, nor did they have a dislike of meat, of any variety. Within the confines of the Cenobium, it was true that the devout were all female and were respectful of life, but they ate healthily, merely adding the occasional rabbit or tree rat to their diet of vegetables and fruit.

As Codrina regained her voice, she faced a pounding of questions by her friend, and by other visitors. Why was she on the sea? Was she travelling alone, how was she shipwrecked? Where did she come from, and what was home like? Was she worried for her parents? Karişkir still refused to believe that Codrina was not a warrior, and nothing could be said to dissuade her friend that she had not single-handedly defeated a band of pirates only to have been overcome by a sea dragon. In one way, Codrina thought, this was not too distant from the truth, although perhaps a little tame.

After some ten days had passed, Codrina was able to walk at last. Her hair had grown the longest since she was eight. Tentatively, she visited the privy chamber, pleased to avoid using the bedpan. Afterwards, every time she crouched to pass her waters she was reminded of her former life. When she was a little stronger still, she was overjoyed to leave the confines of the infirmary. She marvelled at the spectacular views from the safety of the terrace overlooking the ocean far below. She had taken to sitting there each evening to watch the setting sun, while enjoying the echoes of canticles floating from the chapel during vespers, accompanied by the percussion of distant crashing waves. Beautiful pink blooms born on hardy shrubs, clung to the nearby crags and poked through the open balustrade. They opened their petals when the sun set, filling the air with a heady perfume. Clouds of bright-winged moths thronged the flowers' gaping mouths, in turn attracting hungry bats which came to feed as darkness fell.

'Do you mind if I disturb you?' asked Mother Elder one evening, her soft footsteps approaching across the terrace.

Codrina removed her feet from the chair where they had been resting. 'Of course,' she replied, brushing the seat free of imaginary dirt.

'I have been waiting for you to gain your strength,' Mother Elder said, settling down so that the sun instantly began to set over her shoulder. Codrina shaded her eyes from the orange glare which shone like an aura around the figure in front of her. 'I think we have both been patient,' Mother Elder added finally. It was almost a question, but cleverly neutral and saturated with meaning. Codrina had been expecting a conversation, but not considered it would be initiated so directly. She cleared her throat, taking a sip of water while deciding how to respond.

'Let me help you,' began Mother Elder, before Codrina had replaced the beaker on the table by her side and swallowed her last mouthful. 'I think you were sent to us, I think you know more than you have told us, and I believe you have something to ask of us.'

Codrina thought a moment before replying. 'You are wrong on two counts,' she replied quietly. 'As to the third, it's only come to light since I have learned more about this place from Karişkir.'

Mother Elder sat in silence long enough for Codrina to raise her hand again so she could peer within the silhouette before her. The look on Mother Elder's shadowed face was one of disbelief. And still the woman held her tongue.

'You have shown me a rare kindness and more friendship than I thought possible,' whispered Codrina. 'I have you all to thank for my life.'

The figure in front of her nodded once in confirmation of the simple truth. Codrina took a deep breath before continuing. 'It's difficult for me to trust anyone, and to speak the truth. I'm sorry,' she added, 'but that's just my nature.'

'Let me say this,' Mother Elder said softly in return, pausing long enough that her words almost became the buzz of night-bugs and the roar of the ocean.

Codrina found herself leaning forwards, looking intently at Mother Elder. Her face had gained some features now that the lanterns of the terrace no longer competed with the setting sun.

'You have met one of us before, you have known a sister of the Cenobium.'

Codrina nodded slowly.

'Our sisters rarely travel beyond Leybosque, and only ever when on a mission of exceptional importance. I believe you met one of our sisters in your home country.'

Again, Codrina nodded.

'I believe this sister was sent to protect you. Would you like to tell me her name?'

Codrina swallowed. It was a person that no one else had ever known about, and a name she had never even said aloud. 'Her name ...' started Codrina, hesitating.

'Go on,' urged Mother Elder, leaning forward to hold Codrina's hand.

'Her name was Komorebi.'

A gasp escaped Mother Elder, before her shoulders heaved. Codrina was surprised to see tears appear on Mother Elder's cheek. The girl leant forward and gently wiped a tear away with a finger, tilting the balance between the two of them.

'Is she alive?' Mother Elder whispered.

'Yes, at least, I think she is.'

The two of them regarded each other in silence, and as one tension ebbed away, another more urgent energy began to gather between them.

It is well-known that the roots of a walnut seed grow

half the height of a man before the first shoot will even appear above the ground, the gravity-seeking wood beginning its life by parting the earth. In that way it creates a foundation which prevails for centuries to come, whatever extremes it suffers above ground from storm or saw, wind or wickedness. So it was between Codrina and the sisters of the Cenobium, the germ of the girl watered by the tears of the mother, her development nurtured by her new-found sisters.

EARTH ABSORBS WATER

37

E very dream and hope ran cold as tears, like the half-ruined city was mourning its own tragic demise.

Even after all the dead from the firestorm had finally been buried, the gravediggers worked from dawn til dusk. First to follow in droves were elderly victims among the multitudes of new homeless. Later, a plague swept through the region during the unusually cool and rain-drenched summer, taking with it many of the youngest children. For those digging on the hill it was some mercy that the holes to be made in the sodden ground were small, as many little wooden caskets could be stacked one atop the other in an efficient manner; those of the paupers in the shallowest, and those with a coin or more buried below. Mounds of fresh earth pockmarked the recently expanded burial ground around the stump of the ancient walnut tree. From afar it looked like the rains had disturbed a company of hellion moles from the deep.

Komorebi had exhausted every lead while waiting patiently for half a year, before finally admitting to herself that the child was no longer within the city bounds or anywhere nearby. She had travelled across a vast area of Askraland, visiting every town, village, hamlet, and farmstead within two day's walking distance of Bruachavn. She had asked quiet questions of those willing to talk and those intrigued by the green-dressed stranger; chatting with peasants in taverns, sharing gossip with toll masters, bemoaning the weather with exhausted farmhands struggling to bring in the harvest, and with the gentry touring their estates by carriage. No one had seen, sheltered, or employed a tall thin boy, or noticed a lone young adult carrying an unusual axe.

In an attempt to cheer the spirit of the population, the mayor of Bruachavn had announced that a Wuka tournament would be held later in the year. There seemed little enthusiasm among the people, if tavern talk was any way to judge hearts, which of course it was. More energies were focussed on pondering the horrors of the recent past, and expressing concerns for the winter months ahead and the likelihood of a famine due to the failed harvest. The doom-mongers seemed to delight in repeating old lore marking the Feast of Zetsumetsu, 'if the wind is from the east, expect the teeth of winter's beast.'

With a heavy heart, Komorebi realised she must return to her sisters and report her failure to protect the child. As autumn approached, she slipped quietly from the city where she'd tried so hard to fulfil her mission, and began her long overland journey through Askraland and beyond, including the high passes of the Barren mountains. She was headed towards the place she called home, but knew she faced an uncertain welcome, if she was fortunate to survive the journey.

38

In the beginning, came light and dark.
Where there was, became lightful;
Where there was not, became darkness.

Y ou know of this text?'
'Yes, of course,' answered the 13-year-old girl barely glancing round to look at her questioner. She still felt a little vertiginous, but the view from the window was entrancing. If she leaned out a little, the terrace of the infirmarian was just discernible, yet its stone balustrade and vine-clad pergolas were impossibly, only halfway down towards the shimmering water and sweeping curve of sand visible far, far below. Spring sunshine sparkled from the surface of the White Sea, until dimmed by cloud shadows hurtling across the bay. The pale backs of seabirds wheeled beneath them, catching invisible currents near their nests on the cliff, their screeching calls carried in bursts to the open window by the buffeting wind.

It was the first time that Codrina had been invited to this part of the library. The archival room was reached by ascending 113 spiral steps in the tallest tower of the Cenobium, at the top of which they were met by the thickest oak door the girl had ever seen. Its three locks were tackled with separate keys attached to Mother Elder's belt before she swung it open on well-oiled iron hinges to reveal a round room stacked high with scrolls and books. At its centre lay a large wooden table, covered in manuscripts, one of which Mother Elder was now reading aloud while Codrina tried not to think about the time she had spent afloat on the ocean, which looked so tame from the safety of the Cenobium.

Everyone knew the text. It was universal in every country; at least Codrina imagined this must be so. Her mother had read passages to her by candlelight before bedtime. In the city, its words and phrases carried in hymns, reaching her ears while she sold warm pies in the cathedral close. She'd heard fragments from mourners on the hill of the dead, and in the hurriedly muttered prayers of frightened sailors.

'There are other texts held here, that are not widely known,' started Mother Elder, before pausing to check she had the girl's attention.

Codrina dragged her eyes away from the view and turned to look towards Mother Elder. The deep sleeve of her green habit disturbed a cloud of dust from the windowsill set deep in the thick stone wall. Motes and scantlings began to float through the rays of spring sunshine which streamed into the circular chamber. 'It is a remarkable view, isn't it?' said Mother Elder, motioning Codrina to sit beside her.

39

I t was two quarters before when Mother Elder had promised Codrina that when she had recovered fully and learnt some of their ways, she would induct her into more of the scriptures locked away in the Cenobium. She had hinted that there was information which would come to light that might be of great interest, providing important insights, not just for Codrina, but perhaps for them all.

The autumn had crept up on them slowly, like the sea mists which rolled beneath the Cenobium each morning launching it as a floating sky fortress. Codrina had started to feel herself again and was able to join the sisters in taking advantage of a bumper harvest from the Cenobium's extensive garden. After an unusually dry summer, early autumn rains had been absorbed by the cracked earth before swelling the tree fruits. The girl's appetite was well-matched to the plentiful supply of wholesome food, and she wasn't the only one to notice how she was growing taller and stronger every day.

Under Mother Elder's instruction and with Karişkir's enthusiastic encouragement, Codrina joined in with every aspect of life in the Cenobium. She shared her friend's liking of kitchen duties for the obvious reasons, but most of all she appreciated working outside. The two young women worked together bringing in the plentiful harvest of root vegetables and tree fruit from the allotments. She especially enjoyed the task of climbing the contorted hazel trees in the roundel that surrounded the sacred pool. Karişkir had explained that the downpour of nuts, which they divined by vigorous shaking, added fertility and wisdom to the Cenobium's supply of drinking water which they bottled each day. It remained a frustration to Codrina that she had not yet worked in the fields or coppices, while her axe lay sharpened, oiled, but unused under her bed.

'Why has Mother Elder not allowed me beyond the walls?' Codrina asked her friend one afternoon as they toiled in the orchard, filling another basket with golden pears.

Karişkir paused before replying, fiddling with a stray willow stem poking from the weave of the basket. 'I asked Mother, but she wouldn't say, just told me to stay with you everyday.'

There was something Karişkir was not saying, Codrina was sure of it. She knew the girl well enough to be suspicious of her lowered eyes. 'Is she concerned for my safety?' she asked, stretching over to pull an empty basket between them.

Karişkir's cheeks flushed, but she held her tongue as she picked another two pears and placed them carefully in the bottom of the basket.

'Karişkir?'

'I mustn't...I mean, I swore to Mother Elder that—'

'You can tell me,' Codrina urged, leaning close and adding another fruit to the basket.

'I don't know.'

'What do you mean? You don't know if she is concerned for me, or something else?'

Karişkir sighed and finally looked Codrina in the eyes. 'You must swear by the light, not to let her know that we talked about this.'

'Of course!'

Karişkir rubbed her hands up and down the rough brown apron protecting her green habit. Codrina recognised her nervous gesture, like when Cook had caught her with her hand in the biscuit jar last week. 'I think it's my fault,' she said eventually.

'How can it be your fault, you've not stopped me doing anything.'

'I didn't mean to, it just happened before I knew it.'

'Karişkir, you're speaking in riddles!'

Karişkir sighed, and glanced briefly at Codrina, guilt written clearly across her face. Codrina reached out and squeezed her hand. 'Karişkir, it's alright, just tell me. I won't be angry.'

'I told Mother Elder that you used to dress as a boy, and that you had been hunted.'

Codrina laughed. 'She knows almost everything about me Karişkir. Maybe not about me pissing standing up, but everything important.'

Karişkir looked up, relief visibly sweeping away her worries. 'Really, you mean I've not let you down?'

'No, not at all,' answered Codrina, giving her friend's hand another squeeze.

After a moment, they both turned at exactly the same moment and reached to pick the same luscious pear hanging between them. Swift as an arrow, Codrina swept her other hand from underneath to deflect her friend's move and grabbed the fruit, before Karişkir ducked and attempted to sweep her friend's legs away. Codrina lightly dodged the move and before she knew it, Karişkir lay face-down on the earth with her empty arm twisted behind her back.

The two girls rolled over, collapsing in giggles. Karişkir pulled a blade of grass out her mouth and brushed a lock of red hair back under her headdress. Codrina took a giant bite from the pear before passing it over.

'It's rude to laugh with your mouth full!' Karişkir said. 'It's also not fair that you're so good. You've only been learning the beam two quarters and already you're better than all of us.'

'Except Sister Khe.'

'Sister Khe could just sit on you and kill you!' Karişkir said, taking a bite from the pear.

'Yes, but she's also the quickest and most cunning fighter I've ever seen, despite her size.'

'Mother Elder said you were the best sister she'd ever seen practicing the beam, better even than Komorebi.'

Codrina had been staring across the orchard, looking back towards the Cenobium which was just visible between the thinning russet of the trees. Mention of her spirit mother shocked her. She'd only ever discussed Komorebi with Mother Elder, and had never heard her name mentioned by any of the other sisters.

'But she said that it was better to hide than to fight,' continued Karişkir, oblivious of Codrina's astonishment.

'That's a strange thing to say,' Codrina replied.

'She didn't mean that lightful shouldn't overcome darkness. It was when we were talking about you. She said you weren't ready yet and we must keep you hidden.'

Codrina could no longer hide her surprise and interest. Her friend blushed at the intensity of her green-eyed stare.

'So, she did say something after all.'

'Well, I suppose she did,' Karişkir answered with a sheepish grin.

'So, what did she mean about me not being ready?'

Karişkir hesitated. 'Everyone knows you're a warrior and the best follower of the beam anyone has ever witnessed. Mother said that when you're beam was fully focussed, then you won't need to hide anymore. None of us will.'

'And then what?'

'You will fulfil what's written, of course!'

40

C odrina, have you listened to a word I've been saying?'

The girl jumped as Mother Elder grasped her wrist lightly. She looked away from the open window and into Mother Elder's eyes. 'I'm sorry, but I think I did drift off for a moment,' she said guiltily.

'I worry for you, Codrina. You have carried the burden of a personal tragedy with you most of your life, and glimpsed the horrors of the world's burden more than once, but you have much more to learn. It is important; we both know this.'

'Yes, Mother Elder.'

'I am not seeking an apology, just your focus. You have become very proficient in the physical nature of the beam, but you are far from being ready. You must master its essence so that its spirit shines from within. Only then will you be able to follow the true beam.'

Codrina thought for a moment. 'Did Komorebi follow the true beam?' she asked eventually.

'She does.'

'I'm sorry, I didn't mean—'

'I know you didn't, but she is with us still, I can sense her light. It is weak, given the distance between us, but recently I've become very sure of this.'

Thinking that Komorebi was still alive was something Codrina had not allowed herself to believe, but Mother Elder's certainty sent a warm wave rushing from her heart to her head. 'How does she follow the beam?'

'Like you, she learnt from Khe, and like you she eventually bettered her, though she was older than your thirteen years. Mind you, our sensei carried less weight then!' Mother Elder paused, her eyes smiling as she studied Codrina. 'She also studied hard, although in the beginning I remember sitting at this very table having just as much trouble encouraging her to focus on the scriptures.'

The two of them looked at one another a moment, sharing the joke.

'Mother Elder, I've been wanting to ask you something.'

'Yes, my child, you know you can share anything with me,' replied Mother Elder, leaning towards Codrina. She gently tucked a stray strand of long dark hair back under Codrina's headdress and then offered the girl her hand, palm up on the surface of the table.

'You know about the murder of my parents,' Codrina began, pausing to look at the older woman as she took the offered hand.

Mother Elder squeezed her hand and nodded in affirmation, but kept her lips sealed.

'Something happened that night that I've never shared with anyone, something that I've never understood.'

'I'm sure there were many terrible th—' started Mother Elder.

'No, I mean there was something inside me. When I was in most danger, my fear was replaced by something else. Like anger or rage, but much bigger and ... deeper. More like there was a force inside me that I had to release.' Codrina noticed Mother Elder's intense stare and paused again.

'Go on.'

'It drove me to pick up an insignificant object and hurl it at one of my hunters. I can't really explain what happened next, except that it didn't fly as it should and a strange light shone from its path.'

'And then what?' asked Mother Elder quietly.

'It struck him down.'

'Oh!' muttered Mother Elder. 'Did he get up again?'

Codrina's mind instantly conjured up a vivid memory of what had emerged from the forest soon afterwards, but she had already decided to keep Raunsveig to herself. She shook her head shyly. 'No, I think I killed him.'

'Extraordinary,' Mother Elder said, squeezing her hand hard. 'And what was it that you threw?'

'A walnut.'

A soft empty breath escaped Mother Elder's lips. After a long pause, she released Codrina reaching for a kerchief from the sleeve of her habit, before wiping tears from the young woman's cheeks.

Codrina studied her own hands, running her fingertips over the small indents that Mother Elder's silver rings had left on the back of her hand. Seeing Mother Elder weep made her feel uncomfortable. 'I don't think I meant to kill him, but I—'

'My child,' interrupted Mother Elder, 'you must have no remorse for your act. It was a miracle. You are a miracle, yet so innocent.'

'I'm sorry, I don't understand?'

'And that is exactly why we are here together,' Mother Elder answered, 'and now I have this information of new wonders you have shared with me, it only confirms everything I suspected as soon as you came to us.'

Mother Elder stood slowly, deep in thought, and walked over to the window. Codrina waited patiently as she watched her shoulders tremble slightly under the spread of her headdress. The two women kept silent company for a while, only the breath of the wind moving between them. Eventually, Mother Elder straightened her habit, and tucked her kerchief back into her sleeve. Her shoulders rose and fell several times as she deliberately inhaled deep breathes of sea air.

Mother Elder turned around just as the sun burst from behind another scudding cloud. 'As the dry earth absorbs a flood from heaven, you were sent to us near drowned and taken by the ocean,' said Mother Elder. She spoke with the intonation she normally reserved for the chapel. 'And now ... now you are a seed emerging from the earth before us, ready soon to overcome the darkness, and with the power to spread life and light to the world.'

WATER QUENCHES FIRE

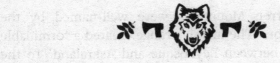

41

The Barren Mountains were well-named by the ancestors. The massive range created a formidable divide between Leybosque and Askraland. To the south they met the White Sea, not delicately as if they were dipping their toes tentatively into its choppy waves, but like they had been amputated at the knees, falling abruptly into the sea in vicious drops of one thousand feet or more. The towering cliffs dwarfed even the Cenobium's celebrated perch above the sea, but the memories and the place itself now lay half a year behind Codrina, who would soon celebrate her fifteenth year. To the extreme north, beyond the territory of Arginta and at the far end of the lengthy spine of mountains, the peaks were swallowed by ice clouds from which no explorer had ever returned, though countless numbers had set out in pursuit of the fabled silver mountain. On a good day, it was said the glittering angles of the mythical peak could be glimpsed from 100 kilomiles to the north.

Legend says that it took one thousand years and one thousand lives before a safe route linking Leybosque and Askraland was discovered through the Barren Mountains.

Now the Upplega Pass was routinely used from late spring til early autumn, but during the remaining months was tackled only by the most hardy travellers and even then, it was essential to hire a guide from among the Barrenese, the indigenous mountain people. Despite the hardships of the lengthy trek, almost all travellers preferred it to a passage across the White Sea, and this was to become a comforting reminder to Codrina as the cold and altitude took their toll on her exhausted body.

On the plains at the western approach to the mountains, prairie vegetation of brush and succulents slowly gave way to scattered trees as the land sloped gently upward towards the distant snow-clad peaks. There were no forests, just scattered isolated trees of spruce and hemlock, scarred and stripped by the vicious wind and cold. The evergreens had too few branches for their height, like a collection of overused paint brushes resting in a pot on the easel of a giant artist, their sparse hairs having barely any impact on the monumental landscape. In the heart of winter they became clad in blobs of frozen snow, as if the artist had forgotten to rinse them clean of porcelain white. These were the infamous 'frozen men' which old tales said were the bodies of previous travellers, frozen upright as they trudged towards the high pass.

Codrina hoped she wouldn't see them herself as it was surely too late for snow, but the idea brought a chill to her body. As her small group of fellow travellers picked their way carefully through the rock-strewn slopes, her mind often turned to memories of the Cenobium. The friendships, hearty food, her lessons in the beam, the discoveries in the archives.

A sequence of three or four easy steps was a simple joy before another obstacle had to be overcome, demanding her full concentration. She would place her stout stick carefully before she manoeuvred her body and the heavy pack on her back around the boulder, or across a tangle of exposed and twisted tree roots. This was no place to twist an ankle. The unwary would never reach the comforts on either side of the forbidding mountain range.

The words of Mother Elder were as fresh in Codrina's mind as when she heard them with her ears, undiminished by the ravages of time that had tried to erode them, nor washed away by recent events which could so easily have cleared her mind of any sense, if not snuffed out her life entirely. Those happy times at the Cenobium, of gentle labour, shared friendship and companionship, and extraordinary physical and mental learning, already seemed a lifetime ago.

In her tent it was still as black as a mine shaft, too early even for the cactus finches and alpine crossbills to declare a new spring day. The canvas flapped slowly in the breeze, reminding her that the wild was still out there, waiting to welcome the weary group for another day of hardship. Codrina rolled over in her bundle of furs, careful not to expose any of her body to the chill. She held her axe close to her chest, but avoided touching any metal exposed between the leather of the sheath and its strapping, as it remained as cold as ice, despite spending the night by her side. Her calves ached terribly and every time she moved her feet, her blisters throbbed. Codrina closed her eyes again, though she could hardly tell if they were open or not, and concentrated on her breathing as she had been taught, hoping it would help her gain some precious moments of sleep. If only she could dream again of Raunsveig, but he had not come to her once since she'd fled Askraland.

The beam had been taught and mastered by countless believers since time began, or at least that's what the oldest scriptures confirmed. It was not called the beam then, simply the light, which modern wisdom suggested was because their ancestors had not yet learnt to fully focus their art. Codrina had spent many hours together with Mother Elder in the archive room at the top of the tower. They had not always been interesting and welcome hours, especially when Codrina knew her friend was working in the garden or even in the coppices, but any early boredom soon gave way to a startling fascination that surged through her mind and body. Working on the beam demanded her undivided attention.

The language of the scriptures was ancient, and even though Mother Elder had studied it for most of her life, she read its passages aloud carefully, her lips often searching silently for meaning before uttering another stilted sentence. Her finger would slowly trace the complex ligatures and elegant looping descenders written in a perfect hand across the vellum. When she reached the end of a passage she would repeat it, this time more fluently before they discussed it together.

Those whom carry light in their soul,
Those whom move against the darkness,
Those for whom self is other, and other is life,
They are the lightful, and they shall walk among us.

The passage from Book I stuck in Codrina's mind, resurfacing in a rhythm strangely attuned to her steps as she wove between the rocks and succulents of the trail. Mother Elder had spoken the words with familiarity, as though she knew them as well as herself.

It was another chilly dry morning and their Barrenese mountain guide, Pastrama, had already coaxed the fire back to life. The familiar smell of boiling oats greeted Codrina as she emerged from her tent. She wiped the sleep from her eyes, and pulling back her green hood a little, savoured the gentle warmth of the rising sun as its rays met her cheeks. A bubbling pot hung from a tripod over the flames, its steam wafting slowly between the tightly-arranged tents. She stamped her feet in the hope some warmth would return to her lower body, before immediately regretting it as needles of pain lanced her soles.

The lean guide hunched over the fire looked up in silent greeting, the wrinkles of a smile creasing his dark tanned face, before returning his attention to the cooking. He wielded his long camp knife skilfully to prepare their breakfast, the same blade that Codrina had witnessed him using to skin mountain hares, chop kindling, and lance blisters. Now Pastrama was using it to shave thin slices of the preserved food they carried with them which the Barrenese called ursgrăsime. The mixture of bear tallow, various powdered meats and dried forest berries dissolved quickly into the porridge. At first it had not sat well in Codrina's stomach, especially after so many moons of a diet consisting only of vegetables and fruit. Now she looked forward to the same food each morning, especially the sensation of warmth that travelled down her insides as she carefully sipped the piping-hot porridge from her wooden spoon.

Codrina was the only one among the four travellers to have risen, and as she balanced carefully on a twisted old pine root to eat her breakfast, she regarded Pastrama as he stirred the porridge a final time and rose to complete other tasks around the camp. He was a man of few words and the words he spoke of the common language were barely understandable through his broken smile. He made himself plain through gestures and the emotions which shone from his startling blue eyes and sharp features. Though he was as thin as the trees that now surrounded them on the slopes, he possessed the strength and endurance of two men. As for Codrina's three fellow travellers, one man was too fond of grain spirit to be capable of much more than putting one from in front of the other, and even that seemed to be a miracle given his excess weight. The other two men were clearly already very familiar with each other. The two characters, who dressed in matching dark cloaks and wide-brimmed hats, kept themselves separate from the remainder of the group. They always spoke in hushed whispers as though something important was about to happen at any moment which only they knew about. Codrina had made it her business to listen stealthily outside their tent, only to discover that they talked endlessly of silver; of silver mining, of the value of silver in the markets of Askraland, and of their grand plans to mount an expedition to the silver mountain.

Codrina cherished some thoughts of silver, including the many rings upon Mother Elder's fingers, the precious gift from Komorebi, and of course the gleaming face of Raunsveig on her axe. Otherwise, her recent experiences in the territory of Arginta and its mines had left her with a vastly different perspective of the precious metal.

With Mother Elder's help Codrina had planned her expedition meticulously. Well fed, fully trained, and armed with new knowledge, the girl would begin her journey home in the company of a caravan benefitting from the safety of strength in numbers, especially through the violent territory of Arginta. They would overwinter together in the western foothills of the Barren Mountains before attempting their transverse in small expeditionary groups during the late spring.

It had not been easy for Codrina to part company with her newfound friends, nor to leave behind the comfortable way of life in the Cenobium. Most of all, for the first time in her life she had felt part of a family and separating from them was the hardest aspect. Tears were shed on both sides when the morning finally came for Codrina to depart. As she headed east along the dusty road leading away from the Cenobium, she looked repeatedly over her shoulder. The three figures of Mother Elder, Karişkir, and the stooped profile of Krummholz, remained visible on the wall above the main gate, lit by the warm glow of the rising sun. She finally lost sight of the Cenobium itself as the track dropped into a shaded wooded valley.

One emotion rose above all others for Codrina. It fed on her passion for good to conquer evil. It was driven by a rage hidden deep within herself which none of her friends even knew existed, and which she could barely dare to think about herself. Codrina simply wanted to return home, she wanted to carry on with the life her father had gifted her, caring for the forest. If she had the chance, she would seek justice. She still felt unsure about many of things she had learnt from her time in the archives with Mother Elder, but nonetheless felt a river of ancient energy coursing through her veins. If the opportunity arose, she had preparedness and allies on her side, especially her three closest friends. Even though they were out of sight, she still felt they were watching over her.

The plan had been perfect in every way, but for the realities of the lawless nature of Arginta, and the weakness in leadership from others who should have known better. Codrina wondered if the leader of the caravan had indeed known better and was awaiting his cut.

They had barely passed its border by a few nights before a well-planned ambush captured the wagon at the rear, which had been left criminally under-guarded. Like many others in the caravan, Codrina lost all her spare luggage containing her winter clothes essential for attempting the Upplega Pass. Her baggage also contained valuable tradable commodities from the Cenobium, including a selection of the finest silks, elegant scrolls of velum with favourite passages of the scriptures fit to benefit the finest home, and some punnets of tiny orangenuts whose rarity always fetched a good price. So, while her coin had been kept safe close around her neck and belt, and her axe was strapped tightly to her back, she had otherwise been robbed of any ability to survive the rest of the journey without earning more funds.

Unable to pay for the tariff for the remaining kilomiles with the caravan without compromising her ability to feed herself, Codrina was forced to stay behind at the next town. It was a miserable place, with unpaved roads ankle deep in red mud, and its wooden buildings consisting of equal numbers of taverns, brothels, and guesthouses, though the latter two were all too easily confused. It had taken several attempts to discover a genuine lodging house, and Codrina left behind several disappointed madams excited by the sight of the fourteen-year-old's bright eyes and long dark hair.

She had spent the next day visiting all three forges in the town, confident that her skills might see her as a welcome addition, but she had been laughed away from every one of them. Each of the burly men had been astonished, merely by the thought of hiring a young girl as a short-term hand, before dismissing her brusquely. One had spared enough effort to suggest she tried any one of the five bakers, but it was soon evident that all of them were overrun by offers from girls anxious to avoid the mines, or worse.

The situation reminded Codrina of a large rock slab worn smooth by the sea under the towering presence of the Cenobium. Once she had regained her health and could tolerate submersing herself in the sea again, Codrina had visited as often as she could with Karişkir. The two girls spent many hours sliding down the gently undulating surface, flying off the small drop at the end and tumbling gleefully into the sea. Sometimes they tried to climb back up the slippery rock, and with every step it felt ever more likely that the feet would disappear under them at any moment, and they would tumble to the bottom. The first few days in the miserable town felt just like the slippery rock. With every perilous step, Codrina felt she would surely loose her step at any moment. In this case, the outcome would be working in the silver mines, although that would be preferable to selling her body.

Surely enough, to keep a roof over her head, keep her body well fed, and save funds towards the continuation of her journey, she soon had little choice but to join a morning queue of casual workers at one of the mines. The coin was good, but came at a price. Miners rarely lived beyond their 30th year, and the last couple of those were normally spent in agony coughing up blood into a kerchief. Codrina spent some precious coin beforehand purchasing work clothes, including a scarf to wear over her face. After enjoying her elegant green cape and loose-fitting pantaloons for so long, she felt like she was once again dressed as a boy, although her long locks and feminine lines would no longer fool anyone. The itchy wool trousers and jacket felt foreign against her skin, but as she centinched towards the foreman at the head of the line, she fitted in perfectly with the drably dressed men, women, and children lined up alongside her, all holding on to the same hope. When her turn came, the foreman felt her body all over with a cruel glint in his eye, checked that her pockets had been sewn closed, looked in her mouth, and welcomed her with a nod and a single word; 'carts.'

She found work every day afterward, spending half a moon underground, mostly pushing the laden carts back towards the surface on their wooden rails. At the end of every shift the older workers spat into their red-flecked kerchiefs as they shuffled home, their teeth shining among the filth of their grizzled faces. Most days, deep underground, she would see the weakened bodies of young and old fainting from exhaustion, left to their own devices as fellow workers struggled on. One time she witnessed a horrific accident when a boy slipped while pushing a fully-laden cart. It rolled over him, cutting through at the ankle, leaving the foot complete with worn-thin sock inside its leather work boot. He lost so much blood, he was dead by the time he reached the surface.

In a neighbouring mine there was worse luck still when the miners struck a pocket of foul firedamp. After the explosion and subsequent collapse of the main shaft, the sluices had to be diverted to quench the ferocious flames which had shot skyward as if Earth herself was roaring. Tragically, 69 miners remained unaccounted for, and black drapes hung from the windows of every tavern until absorbed by the routine misery of the place. Rumours started soon after of a mysterious figure dressed entirely in black who was seen by several witnesses walking between and even through the bodies of many of the missing miners while they had queued for work that morning. Codrina was unconvinced by these tales of fancy, but for several nights afterward she dreamt of Xuan who chased her relentlessly through dark underground tunnels which nearly always came to a dead end, literally and figuratively. She realised that she had not been visited by such dreams while at the Cenobium, and initially they unsettled her more than she could fathom until she realised that she had convinced herself that she was the hunter and not the prey, that she had the upper hand with surprise in her favour. The dreams had shaken that belief and if anything strengthened her resolve to be better prepared and more focussed.

Codrina was managing to save some funds, but they were accruing achingly slowly. In the evenings she joined other miners in one of the many taverns, nursing her blistered hands and easing the aches in her shoulders with a jig or two before consuming a hearty meat pie washed down by a dark ale. Then, one fateful evening, her luck finally changed for the better.

At a nearby table in the especially rowdy Cock and Hen, as Codrina enjoyed her only meal of the day, a raucous game of Wuka was nearing its end. She'd been observing it closely while also conversing with some of her fellow workers whom she had taken to meeting regularly most evenings. The theory of the game, as had been explained to her all those moons ago by the smith, suddenly dropped into place, as snugly as her axe fitted its sheath. She watched the woman playing the Sailor make the fatal mistake of putting too much faith in fate, while a man playing as the Forester thought he was clever, yet any fool could read him like he'd been chopped down, turned to pulp, and made into a book before their eyes. The game came to an end with a victory by an old man playing as Stoker, as she had predicted several rounds before. As he swept the winnings into his cap, the call for new players went out. Before she knew what had gripped her, and to the surprise of her friends, Codrina found herself leaning over and declaring her interest.

And so it was, just two moons later, that a fourteen-year-old girl was banned from playing Wuka in every one of the town's 26 taverns. Her presence near a game only drew gasps of fear, jealously, or worse, and inevitably ended in a brawl through which the tall lithe girl always miraculously escaped unscathed. Her funds burgeoned as rapidly as her reputation. Codrina was soon able to purchase a set of winter furs which looked remarkably like those she had travelled with originally. Her gambling was so successful that she distributed her workwear among her friends and spent her days tutoring Wuka to the hopeful and the desperate, or resting and enjoying an extra meal, before touring the taverns by evening. Within the quarter and with considerable relief, she bade farewell to her surprised friends and joined the next caravan passing east.

45

Karişkir did not exactly gain permission to leave the Cenobium, but then again, in retrospect it was obvious to every single resident, from Mother Elder to the cooks, that there was no way on Earth that the girl could be expected to stay cosseted inside its walls a moment longer.

When her unique friend had left, she was consoled and kept deliberately busy by the community. Collectively they imagined that Karişkir might accept it was best for Codrina to travel alone. They all underestimated the bond which had forged between the two young women.

For the first few nights, Karişkir has cried herself to sleep. From the second week, her dormitory companions considered that her firm resolve, and quiet evenings spent in contemplation were a good sign, indicating her heart and mind had moved on, yet they were greatly mistaken.

In the weeks following, Karişkir was secretly making detailed plans for departure, and gathering the resources needed for the arduous journey. Her increased devotion to the beam was building her strength and physical resilience. Extra hours spent in the archives revealed important knowledge about the terrain to be covered and its peoples.

In the dead of night on her 15th birthday, Karişkir quietly stole away from the Cenobium, without a single glance over her shoulder.

46

'Thill besnore comin downtus day.'

Codrina was dragged from her unpleasant memories of Arginta by the rare comment emerging from Pastrama's ragged mouth. She had become quite used to translating his few words when she had the chance, but repeating them back to him was always best to make sure she had understood.

'There will be snow coming down to us today, did you say?' Codrina asked, their meaning settling on her in the same instant.

The man nodded as a visible shiver ran through him, the consequences for their expedition apparently gripping his own thoughts. He was crouched by the little fire on his haunches, pointing with the porridge spoon towards a blanket of purple clouds hiding some of the high peaks which lay before them. Codrina shifted her half-numb bottom on the gnarly tree root and turned her eyes towards the towering ridge of rock, snow and ice. She wondered to herself whether she would ever make it to the top, let alone safely descend the eastern flanks to reach the fertile countryside of Askraland and the warm spring sunshine of her homeland.

Her fellow travellers emerged noisily from their two tents, alerted by the rare conversation. 'Did someone mention snow was coming?' said the obese one through his hangover, his stinking breath washing over Codrina. Not wanting to inhale for a moment, the girl nodded and looked pointedly in the same direction that Pastrama had gestured to before.

'That'll be a damn inconvenience,' said the man, flapping his arms around his huge belly. 'This trip will be the death of me.'

Codrina considered this for a moment and decided that the man might well be speaking the truth. It was a mercy that she could not read the future and her thoughts were spared the knowledge that only two souls would emerge safely from the eastern side of the Upplega Pass together. The unseasonably late winter refused to loosen its grip. Cold and wet can quench even the brightest fire burning among the fittest souls.

FIRE MELTS METAL

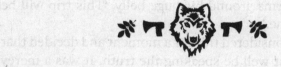

47

Every soul carries light within, though some cast only shade—you will know the sort I'm sure. Their focus is on self not others, they hold a gloom all round themselves, the sort you might catch if you were to get too close. Their eyes are dull and mistrustful, their words miserable and evil, their spirit sucking joy and wonder from everything and everybody. They live for mastery over others, rather than of their own lives. They think only of themselves and the now, not of others and the hereafter. These are the people who threaten to drag us down, down towards darkness, oblivious to their hand in ending the life of another, their role in voiding creation itself. On such people the lessons of the beam would be wasted, unless they discover first their own epiphany. But you my child, you are of the other sort, a soul within which the light is barely concealed. It shines from your eyes and in the flow of your limbs. It glows, sizzles, and sparks inside you like iron within a blazing forge. Think of me as a smith if you will, and in my hand, I am forging a blade of light fashioned from you. The blade will be brighter than all that have ever been before. It will dazzle and shine more brightly than the sun, banishing all shadow, fear, and misery. The eyes of every creature on Earth will turn towards you to bask in the warmth of your rays. Your beam will conquer darkness and once again, the world will be lightful.'

Mother Elder's words still seemed a little fanciful to Codrina as she wiped the ice from her eyelashes and peered out from the furs of her bed roll, squinting against the brightness. Careful not to expose any of her body to the cold, she rolled towards the tent entrance and peeped out between a gap in the stiff canvas and its frozen lacing. She was relieved beyond belief to see the early morning sun breaking through the cloud cover which had smothered the pass for the previous seven days. Light dazzled from every facet of ice like a thousand broken mirrors, reflecting brightly from the little clouds of steam which escaped her lips as she gasped in the freezing air.

The top of the pass lay behind them by half a day. Like all of the little group, Codrina had been looking forward to the end of the relentless ascent, but within an hour of reaching the eastern flanks of the pass, her thighs were aching and the soles of her frozen feet smarting with every downward step. A careless moment by the big man had nearly dragged them all over the edge of an abyss, but for the quick thinking of Pastrama. The guide managed to anchor himself to the ice with his metal-spiked staff and stopped them all sliding down one after the other. In Codrina's mind, the rope that linked them together reminded her of line fishing in the White Sea, but in a strange, inverted way. It was like she was a fish, lured and tethered, and likely at any moment to be dragged below to the frozen depths. She vowed to keep her knife within instant reach on her belt in case she might need to sever the line in a hurry.

She could hear others stirring in their tents. It was too cold to attempt a fire and they would all need to rise quickly together and get moving. She sliced a generous portion from the ball of ursgräsime she kept in a leather pouch on her belt and crammed the cold slice into her mouth, before making a vigorous start to breaking camp before her fingers froze.

48

Karişkir relished her freedom. She carried herself with a rare air of confidence, and her affable ways meant she made friends at every village and town. Trouble and threat rolled off her like water from the back of a Barrenese merganser. Only in the town of Arginta did she feel any discomfort, and even then, mostly in empathy because of the appalling conditions endured by the miners and the young women.

Codrina's trail was far from cool, even though Karişkir had started several quarters behind her friend. In Arginta especially, her friend had made quite an impression and Codrina's name surfaced regularly in the taverns, especially during any game of Wuka. Karişkir had never played yet listened intently when her friend had described it to her in considerable detail. She couldn't pretend to fully understand its complex rules, but she grasped the concept of the five elements and how they interplayed with different characters.

It seemed that Codrina had spent some time in Arginta, evidently earning money by playing and teaching the game. Why she had done this remained a mystery, as Karişkir had helped pack her bags with goods of great value so that she would not have to beg or borrow.

Karişkir waited only a half a quarter for a place with next group heading over the Upplega Pass. She was definitely catching up with her friend. Talk was that the last group to leave had met with unseasonably late snowfall, but it was led by one of the most experienced Barrenese guides, so most folk expected them to have made the passage successfully. Karişkir wondered whether Codrina had been part of that unfortunate party, or whether she had crossed much earlier and was already enjoying the spring sunshine of Askraland.

49

Far below, the little figure was making slow progress ascending the steep pass. It was rare to see one attempting to make the crossing alone, let alone this early in the season.

He had been here long, long ago, but the land had changed little in that time. It was good hunting territory, although he could not bear the brightness of the place with his own body at this time of year. He had not trusted any of his followers to pursue her trail as there was nowhere to hide, especially from an alert and intelligent quarry.

Unlike the western flanks of the mountains, here to the east the scattered pine trees extended well above the snowline. There had been an unusually late fall of wet snow which smothered the trees in capes like frozen white travellers.

Xuan observed the woman searching for one hidden cairn after another, the usually well-worn trail blanketed with fresh snow. She stumbled occasionally, each time struggling to stand before heaving her bundle of possessions onto her back again and feeling her way forward, thrusting her staff here and there to probe the snow.

The temptation to strike while her guard was down, was tempting indeed. Even from afar it was obvious her body was ravaged by her travail which only made a successful outcome more likely. He had been unusually restrained, but then he knew it was an investment likely to swing fortune in his favour. The green-clad one had been graced by luck and not a little skill in evading him for longer than he cared to contemplate. But now, his pertinacious patience and cunning would surely deliver the ultimate outcome, if his senses were proven true. He was increasingly convinced that the woman would lead him to his ultimate quarry. While he might regret missing the satisfaction of a personal confrontation, his success would cast darkness far and wide. It would mark the end for those who dared to stand against him, and the beginning of the foreshadowed era of nihility.

50

K omorebi was exhausted, her limbs stiff with cold. She had not expected so much snow. When she had last passed the same route, travelling the opposite way, her heart had been full of excitement—plus a healthy measure of trepidation—for the mission which then lay before her. It had buoyed her step and washed the exertion from her mind. Now only grit and fear fuelled her slow progress as she climbed the steep slopes marking the final approach towards the top of the pass, perhaps just one more day's climb away. Beyond, it would feel like downhill most of the way, though the Cenobium lay many weeks beyond.

The high ridge and its chink which marked the top of the pass had been hidden by sullen clouds for days on end. Earlier that morning she had woken in her snow-hole with a deep chill, but was relieved to feel the weak spring sunshine on her face, and even happier when she spotted that the way ahead was visible at last. At first, as she shielded her eyes from the bright blue sky and squinted into the distance, she believed there was a scattering of dark rocks further up the route. As the day wore on however, she became ever more convinced the tiny black specs were a group of people travelling the opposite direction, descending from the high pass towards her.

She'd not had company, nor even seen another soul for the past ten days, though she couldn't shake the feeling that she was being watched. On occasion it had caused her to turn around abruptly, thinking she might catch a pursuer unawares, but there was never anyone there. In any case, there was nowhere to hide now that she was crossing the featureless snowfield about the tree line. But still the feeling persisted, and she had lain awake much of the night, unable to shake the sinistrous sense of foreboding.

The two parties continued to close on one another during the day. Surely the other group, who Komorebi could now see numbered five, would by now have spotted her lone figure climbing towards them. She judged that they might reach each other before nightfall, though on this side of the ridge a deep shadow would engulf the path well before sundown. Her feet no longer sunk deep into powder snow, but crunched through a crispy crust of surface ice crystals. Her steps lengthened with renewed vigour.

Komorebi's eyes became fixed on the way ahead and her mind focussed on the prospect of some company, and perhaps a little comfort, as the group would surely be better equipped and supplied. If she had once again turned round to look over her shoulder, she would have been distracted by a mass of dark clouds rapidly massing behind her in the otherwise ice-blue sky.

51

Now that the skies were clear, the view eastwards from the main ridge of the Barren Mountains was truly spectacular. Somewhere, far in the distance lay Askraland, and deep within its fertile forests nestled her birthplace. By the time Codrina reached its rolling hills and lakes, spring would have arrived in all its glory, and life would be bursting forth.

Her mind was lost in pleasant thoughts when Pastrama shouted back to her over his shoulder, pointing forward with the icepick of his mountain staff. 'Thersomun cumin frumbulo!'

'Really! exclaimed Codrina in surprise.'

Her travelling companions asked what the guide had said. 'There's someone coming from below,' Codrina repeated.

The guide nodded without turning round, spitting a gob-full of chewed black leaves onto the snow. She stepped carefully over the steaming mass and joined the others crowding round Pastrama straining to follow the direction of his pointing staff.

Sure enough, the dot of a lone figure was visible far below, its dark shadow many time larger than the body itself. It would be the first person they had seen outside their group for countless days and there was bound to be news to share. It was unusual for anyone to travel alone, and for the rest of the morning and into the afternoon, there was little other topic of discussion among the group. Occasionally, as they descended through gullies, traversed knolls and zig-zagged down precipitous sections, their faces held close against the rock and ice, they momentarily lost sight of the diminutive figure. Yet every time their visibility was re-established, the two parties had edged a little closer to one another. It seemed increasingly likely they would meet before nightfall.

As the afternoon drew on, a feeling of lightness gripped the little group, fuelled by relief now that they had covered the most arduous sections of the route. There was also the simple joy of sunshine and the distraction of the mystery traveller which eased the exertion. The shadows lengthened and their group was eventually cast under the shadow of the ridge high on their right side, even while a brilliant blue sky remained above them. Only a single dark cloud hovered in the distance, beyond the lone traveller.

'I don likat clud!' Pastrama said quietly to Codrina, as they enjoyed walking side-by-side down an easy section of the route.

'Did you say you don't like that cloud?' Codrina asked, wondering if the others had heard, but their party was strung out across the rock-strewn route, now that they were no longer roped to one another. 'It is strangely dark, isn't it?'

'Weshud finsheltur.'

Codrina looked around and pointed speculatively to a snow-free outcrop mid-way between their group and the approaching figure. Its gentle overhang would provide some shelter in the event of a snowstorm, or even heavy rain.

Pastrama nodded silently before raising two fingers to his lips and releasing a long and piercing multi-toned whistle. He gazed intently at the figure below, waiting expectantly for a return message in the curious long-distance language of the Barrenese. They were met by silence although the figure raised an arm in salute. The traveller was clearly not a mountain guide, which had been the most likely theory discussed between the group for most of the day.

Codrina noticed something else unusual about the figure which was only obvious when they had waived their hand. It appeared as though they wore a cloak, not the tight-fitting fur suits common among all the guides and travellers who dared to cross the Barren Mountains while winter still bared its teeth for one final bite at the living.

52

Karişkir thought the lower slopes of the Barren mountains were the most alien landscape she had ever experienced. The plants were unlike any she'd seen before, the dry hills seemed incapable of sustaining life, while the strangeness of nights without the constant sound of the sea still unsettled her.

One morning, she had watched intently as her Barrenese guide removed the spines from several leaves of a succulent and pressed them by sitting on them while she cooked their breakfast. The milky white exudate dripped from carefully pierced sides, before collecting in a flat dish. It was then placed among the smoke of the fire until it had dried to a powder.

Her group of six travellers was by good fortune, well assembled. All were fit and able, and together they made a merry crew. The good company helped the kilomiles pass more easily, despite the constant fatigue in her legs.

In the evening before the group reached the snowline, their guide filled her clay pipe with some black leaves and a sprinkling of the white powder, before passing it round.

The next morning, Karişkir remembered little of the night. She had a fuzzy memory of a night of great merriment. She vowed not to imbibe again, in fear that next time her possible humiliation might be much worse. In any case, the toughest section of the pass lay before them, and Codrina lay close beyond. Now she had stay focussed and keep her wits about her.

53

One moment the distance remained too great to
discern any details, while in the next, the unequal
parties approached one another.

Both parties had lost sight of the other as Codrina's
party scrambled over and round a particularly steep
section of the route near the outcrop. The drop was
precipitous, and none of the travellers dared to rush,
placing one foot carefully in front of the other, backs
pressed hard against the rocks. When both parties
reappeared, their figures were immediately obvious to one
another.

For a moment they regarded each other, before a cry
escaped Codrina's lips and she leapt forward. She ran along
the widening ledge towards the lonely figure with a green
cloak matching her own.

'Komorebi,' she whispered between sobs, hugging the
woman as she were her own mother.

'Codrina, my grown child,' came the soft reply.

The last moment Codrina remembered clearly was
glancing over her shoulder and reading the looks of

surprise on the faces of her travelling companions. For all four of the men, their last moments of life were blessed by the joyous grin of a young woman with sparkling green eyes.

Immediately, every hair on their bodies began to tingle and rise.

54

A darkening bolt shot suddenly from the ominous cloud which in its final approach had accelerated towards the travellers with unnatural speed. Its tremendous flash obliterated light from the entire mountain in an instant, while a clap of thunder like no other simultaneously shook the ground.

In the resulting void, a green light erupted from the pair of women, casting an eerie glow round the still-embracing figures.

A second bolt came, then a third, so close behind that light did not return to the scene between their dark flashes.

It was in the moment when darkness briefly reigned supreme when a brilliant beam of green shot skyward. The lightful energy led directly from Codrina's outstretched hand, striking up at the heart of the cloud.

As suddenly as it had begun, the scene returned to how it had been, moments before. Above the barren mountainside, the paling blue sky was completely cloud free. Once more, weak afternoon sunshine lit the mountains, though nothing was as it had been.

Among the icy boulders and pockets of snow lay the

remains of four bodies, frozen in motion as black ash. All the possessions of the male travellers had been combusted along with their fragile lives, but for the remains of belt buckles, cooking utensils, and the ice picks of their walking staffs, which lay round them as globules of molten metal, still sizzling on the frozen ground.

METAL CHOPS WOOD

55

The babbling of the brook chimed with the bright chirping of a flock of chiffingchaffs bobbing through the branches. Close by, the white heads of flowering icicledrops poked through cushions of bright green moss trembling in anticipation of spring. The gentle sleeping breaths of Komorebi melded with the gentle breeze. Codrina watched the woman's chest rise and fall, her exhalations making little clouds which played across a single ray of dawn sunshine stretching towards them through the forest.

The two women had spent another night lying close together under a shared bundle of capes and an odd assortment of garments in a vain attempt to keep the cold at bay. Codrina studied the gentle curved nose and delicate lips of her companion, recalling the many times that Komorebi had been there for her. Codrina had once regarded Komorebi as her spirit mother, but recent events had changed their relationship dramatically.

A week had passed since the atrocious affray, high on the eastern flanks of the Upplega pass. In the immediate aftermath, the two friends were distressed and alert in equal measure. While Codrina strode across the scorched scene, staring in shock at the scant remains of her little party, Komorebi had been unable to take her eyes off the tall figure of her friend. When she had last seen Codrina she had been dressed as a gangly boy hiding among the shadows of Bruachavn. That vulnerable youth had blossomed into a confident young woman; a woman who moments before had conducted a miracle grander than any recorded in the ancient scriptures.

The tragic loss of life dulled the brightness and wonder of their initial meeting. The immediate threat of another attack meant that they talked little as they covered the four bodies with piles of blackened stones, their own hands and feet becoming marked with deathly ashes. There was no discussion as to their next steps; independently both knew what must be done. They turned their backs on the scene and on the pinnacles surrounding the high pass, now glowing orange in the final moments of that fateful day, and together headed eastward down the mountainside.

During the days which followed, they talked with hardly a pause as they descended side-by-side into the increasingly dense pine forests, making their way towards the border with Askraland. Komorebi wanted to know every detail of Codrina's extraordinary passage across the White Sea, and she especially enjoyed news of her old friends in the Cenobium. Codrina listened with regret as she learned of Komorebi's frantic search for her, and of the terrible conditions in the city following the firestorm.

Eventually, Komorebi tentatively broached the topic of the mountainside incident, unsure whether Codrina would want to talk about it. 'I hadn't known you'd reached the Cenobium and received any training. Even if I had, I would still have been surprised. I've never seen a force conjured forth like that!'

It was noon and they had paused together on the crest of a gentle ridge in the foothills. Behind them lay their long arduous descent and beyond the high ridge of the mountains stretching end-to-end across the horizon. In front of them, forest stretched as far as they could see, rolling in gentle waves like a green ocean lapping at their feet.

'But you brought the beam alive too,' Codrina answered, without taking her eyes from the apple she was quartering with her knife.

'We created a shield together, and it saved our lives,' Komorebi said, before continuing hesitantly. 'But you achieved something wondrous. Where did you learn to cast a beam like that? It had such power!'

'I don't know.'

'Well, I'm certain it wasn't from Sister Khe.'

Codrina answered with a small shake of her head, before passing two quarters of the apple to her inquisitor.

'I assume Mother Elder knows?'

Again, a small nod from the young woman, before she looked up into Komorebi's eyes. 'Its power scares me a little.'

'It is a wonder. A force for good to overcome any evil,

including whatever it was that we faced together on the mountain. That was darkness from the most evil of sources.'

Codrina said nothing, turning her eyes to the verdant view, allowing the warmth of the sun to warm her face. Komorebi crunched her apple and offered a hardtack in return.

'In truth, these biscuits will break my mouth!' exclaimed Codrina.

The two chuckled briefly and sat for a few moments in silence. After some time, Komorebi took hold of Codrina's hand. 'What did Mother Elder share with you?'

Codrina sighed, as if the memory was too great a burden.

'Would you rather I didn't question you so?'

'No, it's simply that by speaking of what I've been told will only confuse me further. Truly, I find it difficult to accept as the truth.'

Komorebi squeezed her hand tighter. 'Maybe it will help if you share it with me.'

'Perhaps.'

The mews from a pair of mountain buzzards riding the currents high above the hills echoed through the trees. Codrina took a big breath and placed her free hand over Komorebi's and began to tell her what she had learnt from the ancient scriptures with Mother Elder.

Codrina rose early and started a modest fire while Komorebi slept fitfully in the mossy hollow that had nestled them through the night. They had no pots to boil water for chi or to cook with, but since reaching the forest they had concocted a tasty solution. There was a common mushroom which grew on the stems of fallen pines. It toasted well on a stick and tasted even better with an added slice of ursgrăsime which melted deliciously into the gills. Codrina completed two of the snacks and put them to keep warm on a flat stone near the fire edge before glancing again at Komorebi.

Her friend was awake and clearly had been watching her intently for some time. As Codrina looked up, she eased herself upright and straightened her habit, tucking loose locks of hair inside her headband. 'Good morrow,' Komorebi said wearily.

'I think you travelled far in your dreams!'

'Oh, did I speak out?' asked Komorebi.

'No, but your body flinched most of the night.'

'I'm sorry if I ruined your slumber. I was visited by the same horrors which have haunted me every night since the mountain.'

'They will pass.'

'Oh, I am sure of that!' replied Komorebi, especially as last night everything changed.'

'Really?' Codrina asked, carefully lifting another piping hot mushroom from her stick.

'Your words of yesterday. They have filled my waking and sleeping mind ever since.'

'Oh,' Codrina said quietly, watching Komorebi wipe

sleep from her eyes with a finger.

'Your rings!' exclaimed Codrina suddenly, pointing at her friend's hands with her toasting stick. 'Where are your rings?'

'I no longer wear them, that is all.'

'But you had so many elegant rings!'

Komorebi simply nodded, her eyes staring intently at the flames between them. The fire crackled and flared bright orange as drops of melting ursgrăsime dripped from her toasting mushroom. 'Of course, I've heard of the Legend of Parousia, everybody has. Yet I venture no one believes in it more than any other tale of old.'

'Perhaps,' answered Codrina, just as evasively.

'But what you unearthed with Mother Elder is extraordinary! If anyone else had told me, I would not have believed them.'

Codrina reached round the fire and offered Komorebi the hot mushroom still on its stick, before helping herself to one from a warming stone. In unison, both women blew on their tasty morsels and popped them whole into their mouths. They juggled the hot food on their tongues, grimacing and puffing out their cheeks, before grinning stupidly at each other.

Komorebi wiped the grease from her lips with the back of her hand. 'In truth, that's the best food I've had in a long time.'

Codrina smiled proudly, setting up another on her charred stick.

'You shouldn't be modest. It is a miracle. No, more than that, you are a miracle!'

Codrina looked up and was taken aback by the look of intensity on Komorebi's face. 'I thought for a moment you were talking of the mushrooms!'

'The legend speaks of a child who will walk the earth and banish evil. I have never heard anyone, anywhere, tell of a version where this was a girl. I don't believe it's a fact which could ever be forgotten or changed, even over the eons since our ancestors first wrote it down.'

'Mother Elder took me to the locked room in the tower and read from the original. It took her a long spell to decipher the words.'

Komorebi gasped. 'I didn't know an original even existed!'

Codrina started to recite the familiar passage from Roots, and Komorebi joined with her, their words resounding between the pines.

> *They are the lightful, and they shall walk among us.*
> *Together they shall teach the light, and carry the light.*
> *Until the day of parousia comes,*
> *When there shall be born from the heart of trees,*
> *A child to conquer evil.*

'In all the copies Mother Elder showed me in the archives, even truly ancient scriptures written in the oldest hand, this is the entirety of the famous passage. Mother Elder told me that she had spent two whole quarters studying the scriptures and searching the archives. It was dark in the room, but for our candles. She walked over to a wall panel by the shelves which looked much like all the others, but when she pressed on it in a certain way, it swung open. She placed both hands deep inside and from the shadows withdrew a long wooden box with a curved lid. When she brought it to the table, I could see it was made from the finest walnut. My eyes were drawn to its beautiful figure. In the flickering candlelight, its swirls of dark peat and gold ore glowed brightly, revealing motes of sun-flares and galaxies of dark stars.'

Komorebi gasped. 'Had she discovered it before?'

'She said only the day before, but at that time her eye had been drawn to the many interesting scrolls hidden alongside it. She came to me well before dawn that day, the candle trembling in her hand as she gripped my shoulder, urging me to rise from my bed and to go with her. She said a wolf had spoken to her in a dream.'

'A wolf?'

'Yes, I have seen him too. I will tell you about him, but later?'

Komorebi nodded.

'Mother Elder showed me a wooden key round her neck. Then she told me, "All Mothers have worn this key since time began, but I don't know how many have known its secret."'

'I have seen it, round her neck! Go on,' urged Komorebi.

'The key slotted perfectly into the lock of the box. Inside, wrapped in furs, was the oldest roll of velum I have ever seen.'

A sudden burst of orange sparks alerted Codrina that a mushroom had dropped off her stick and fallen into the fire.

'Never mind!' Komorebi said quickly. 'Why didn't you

tell me this detail yesterday?'

Codrina shrugged.

'Well, what was written?'

Almost in a whisper, Codrina continued her story. 'Mother Elder's hands shook, and her lips trembled. She began to decipher the words, letter by ancient letter. I left the table for a while and went over to the window to gaze at the stars, allowing her to continue her study. Just as dawn began to light the eastern horizon of the White Sea, she called for my attention. Then she spoke the words which filled my mind and the room with brilliant light. I can't remember any other part of that day, yet the words in those four lines shall never leave me.'

She shall generate in her soul the beam of life,
And grow to overcome the darkness.
Her given name and being shall be of the forest,
Her name shall be Codrina.

56

Bosquillas del Argintas had once been a prosperous if brutal frontier town, built on the riches of silver mining before the deposits were exhausted. Desperate investors and miners, and their hungry families, clung on to the vain hope of another strike, but their efforts yielded only lead and zinc. Then a clever alchemist had discovered the green gold to be found within every tree, so now the town was enjoying a new boom. Grand houses were under construction, three storeys high even a kilomile away from the town centre. Paved roads led all the way into the main square which benefited from a gleaming town hall made from engineered wood, five grand banks with timber colonnades, plus numerous bustling cafés and smart taverns.

Codrina and Komorebi enjoyed a hearty meal in a tavern several streets away, relieved to find it had beds spare in the upstairs rooms. It was one of the original taverns; draughty, filthy, low ceilinged, and noisy. They selected it for its roaring fire, honest people, raucous atmosphere, and the likelihood of a good game or two of

Wuka. Before their meal, the two of them had already taken wins at every table, which was fortunate as they could now afford to pay for the hearty broth. They hoped that a fresh intake of unenlightened would allow them to earn more coin later in the evening. That was before they were interrupted by a pair of men, who without invitation dumped themselves on the long bench opposite.

'And what might two young ladies be doing in a place like this?' said the larger of the two as he slammed his tankard clumsily onto the table.

'We thought we might take your coin!' Codrina replied quickly.

The pair looked each other, eyebrows raised in surprise, before roaring in laughter.

The men proved to be better company than their entrance had threatened. They quizzed the women about where they had come from, although it was obvious they recognised the green cloaks of the Cenobium. Codrina's regalement of the trek over the snow-bound Upplega Pass earned both of them a free ale. In return, the men told them about life in the region, the most distant from the great city of Bruachavn. They eventually agreed to a game of Wuka, but after a clean sweep by the women—Codrina played the Forester and eventually beat Komorebi as the smith—the two men had enough sense to refuse another game.

Talk turned back to the forests which gave the men their livelihoods. With a nervous glance sideways, the smaller of the two, who suffered from terrible acne on his cheeks, lowered his voice and leant forward. 'If you're heading east, mind how you go. I would avoid being out late, in the dark like.'

'Why's that? Komorebi asked brightly, casting a quick look at her friend.

'There's been strange goings on, that's all. Folk disappearing, women 'specially.'

'Really?' Codrina replied, trying to sound surprised, even though her stomach knotted.

'They've found bodies in the woods, burnt black like Queen Alfredo's cakes. They say—'

'These two fine ladies won't be wanting any more of your gossip now, Nathan. Leave them be,' interrupted the bigger man suddenly, his face scowling briefly. He wiped his big hands on his thighs before relaxing, but not without obvious effort. 'Why not tell them about the tournament instead?'

'Right. Well, there's a silvan tournament, not three days from here. We were thinking we might try our hand at it. A poster I saw mentioned there was one thousand coin to be won!'

'Is that right?' replied Codrina with feigned disinterest, confident that Komorebi was reading her thoughts.

Later that evening in the privacy of their room, they enjoyed their first beds for countless nights. The two women talked about the tournament, agreeing that it would be a fitting tribute to her late father if Codrina were to display some of her woodsman skills. It would also be a great venue to tour during the evening with the aim of winning a little more coin.

Codrina's mind refused to allow sleep to carry her

away. Judging by the snores coming from the next bed, Komorebi had no such trouble. She wondered why there might be more murders in a region so far distant from the city, and why women were being targeted. She also knew the answers to these questions all too well, and her mind only raced faster. Codrina dissected her journey across the Barren Mountains and their thwarting of Xuan's darkening bolt. The memory of the black-ash figures of her travelling companions was swept up in imagery of forests and burnt mushrooms. She strode through a vast forest whose trees got closer and taller with every step, eventually stealing all the light. Something stirred ahead. Twigs snapped and foliage rustled. She threw herself down into the leaf litter, and peered up towards the swaying tree canopies.

Directly over her head, jaws open and teeth glistening, Raunsveig gazed down at her. His bright eyes searched her soul. Carried by a warm earthy geosmin, his words reached out towards her. 'I'm coming for you,' he growled in the deepest rumble. Codrina smiled and lost herself in the comfort of his companionship.

57

The discovery of the four bodies, hidden under piles of blackened stones near a prominent rocky outcrop, had been a sobering experience for Karişkir and her party as they descended from the high pass. With dread, the young woman had removed enough stones from the first of the graves, hoping with all hope that she wouldn't discover a face she recognised. What she found was almost as disturbing. The burnt bone fragments and black ash were barely recognisable as human remains, but a collection of items with the body and a posse of fresh mountain flowers suggested the bodies had not long been buried. Karişkir checked the other three graves, only to discover all were the same. None of the items interned with the bodies offered any clues, being common utensils or equipment used by those traversing the pass.

All in the group were mystified as to how so many travellers could have died in one place and how their bodies have been cremated so efficiently. There were no signs of any funeral pyres, only a large blackened circle around the bodies. Measuring 50 paces across, everything inside its perimeter had been burnt, melted, or covered in a fine black ash. Everywhere that is except in one small area near its centre, barely large enough for one or two people to stand. Curiously, the mountain grasses were bright green and dotted with the nodding white flowers of mountain saxinage, whilst all round them life had been extinguished.

Karişkir knelt in the centre of the green patch and closed her eyes while she offered some words of light for the lost souls. As she opened them and dried her tears, her something glinted within the foliage. She reached forward and with her green-painted nails, plucked the tiny object from among the mountain grasses.

She gasped as she recognised it as part of the silver clasp which all Cenobites wear to hold their cloaks at the front. It could mean only one thing; Komorebi or Codrina had passed this way. She cut off a lock of red hair, and while the rest of the group brewed some chi, she platted a bracelet to hold the silver fragment safely on her wrist.

58

The trappings of the silvan tournament lay below them, sprawled across a beautiful fertile valley surrounded on two sides by steeply rising woods of oak and other hardwoods. Tents of every design and colour, their feet buried by a soft morning brume, were scattered far and wide, becoming increasingly tightly packed towards the centre of festivities where a large clearing stood ringed with flags and gonfalons.

Codrina and Komorebi descended from their vantage on the ridge and followed a slow meandering river flanked by pussy withies, its waters alive with trout darting between beds of bright green watercress. The river's banks carved a sinuous parting through emerging flowers of sedge, meadow flag, and bloodwort. Dozens of heavy horses were tethered around the fringes of the tents, and judging by their slops they were enjoying the lush grass. Nearby, a pair of giant walnut trees straddled a wide berm protecting them from winter waters while allowing their hungry roots to reach the fat and fruitful earth.

The two women passed among the slow-rising competitors and onlookers, before threading through the small marquees of food purveyors, their grates still warming in readiness for breaking fast. There was a quiet bustle at the confluence of the site. Hazel hurdles were being erected to control anticipated crowds, and nearby the final adjustments made to a semi-circle of tables arranged around the outside of a central ring. Codrina approached a man directing activities to enquire about registration and was dismissed with a wave towards a tall conical tent on the outskirts.

The tent was flanked by two gonfalon depicting a tree and forester in red and silver, and a door in its striped canvas was held open by a carved totem featuring forest animals.

'You're too early!' came a gruff reply from a man bent over a table inside, his face concealed by a green velvet cap.

'We've come a long way—' started Codrina.

'Everyone's come a long way,' he huffed, his eyes finally leaving his ledger to glance briefly at the female before him. 'You're too young, and anyway the women don't compete until the 'morrow.'

'It will be today that I compete.'

'Is that so!' The man's face jerked upwards, focussing again on the young woman in the green cape standing so confidently before him. His eyes scanned her lithe figure before settling on the axe strapped to her back. 'And just what makes you believe you will stand a chance against the men?'

'That is for me to prove and for you to wonder,' replied Codrina calmly, casting a quick glance back to Komorebi who stood at the tent entrance watching the scene unfurl with a twinkle in her eyes.

'Well ... I suppose ... at least you might provide some entertainment,' he blustered. 'I will need to inspect your axes.'

'I have only the one,' answered Codrina. In the blink of an eye the axe was in her hands with such a flourish the man staggered backward a step.

Codrina watched him run his hand along its shaft, checking the axe head for fastness before running his fingers carefully over its gleaming edge, but it was clear that his eyes were drawn to the face of the wolf inlaid in silver on its blade. For a moment he was silent, evidently lost in his own thoughts, before he looked again at the face of the young woman.

Her piercing green eyes held his stare. This was most unorthodox. She would only embarrass herself, young, weak, and wielding her fancy axe. 'So be it,' he found himself saying, before asking for a name to enter in the ledger.

'Whoever declared that a woodsman must be a man,' shouted Codrina over her shoulder as she strode from the tent.

Only Komorebi witnessed the flabbergasted look on the registrar's face. 'Her name's Codrina,' she said, before turning to follow her friend.

Word had spread like wildfire, and round the camps towards the evening of the opening day there was little talk beyond that of the young woman who had passed through the first four rounds to reach the quarter finals on the 'morrow. While her competing against men was itself remarkable, there were more tattle and bruit about a wolf head supposed to mark her axe. Some said the blade flashed green as she swung it, others said it was her eyes that gleamed. Two men even claimed to have been bested at Wuka by the woman and her mysterious friend in a tavern not five nights past, but their stories were disbelieved as fancy. Everyone—woodsman, peasant, and noble—agreed that felling a tree in just three strikes at the first round of the silvan tournament was the sign of a champion to be.

So it was that early next morning, in the mixed forests of oak, maple, and hornbeam on the warm south-facing slopes above the valley, a large crowd gathered impatiently to watch the woman in green continue her passage through the tournament. They were not disappointed. Even though the oaks became larger and gnarlier with each subsequent round, she despatched every one of them as easily as she conquered her fellow competitors.

When the semi-final got underway, early after noon, the competitors were lined up for a formal introduction to onlookers. Her gracile figure was dwarfed by the other three woodsmen who towered over her, their arms larger than her waist. As her name was announced a great cheer erupted from the crowd which had swelled further as time passed. The giant hornbeam trees they faced in the round presented the toughest obstacle so far. Their fluted trunks deflected blows, their contorted grain pinching and snatching at the axe heads, the hardness of their hearts blunting edges faster than any other. The woman in green—her name now on everyone's lips—sailed through like an albatross skimming over the whitecaps of the White Sea while her competitors were tossed around like flightless diving birds.

The grand final was arranged for later in the day, allowing time for the two woodsmen to sharpen their axes, massage their aching limbs, and fuel their bodies for the toughest round yet of the tournament; the ultimate challenge of felling a walnut tree.

Codrina fought her way forward, trying to stick within reach of her fellow finalist. Souchen was a giant of a man with a cape of thick bear fur round his broad shoulders. His silver-decorated ponytail swung from side to side as he responded to the crowd. As he lumbered towards the venue, a weighty axe slung over each shoulder, people swirled in his wake. They pressed in immediately, jostling to gaze upon the young woman close by his back, or even to touch her cloak. Immediately behind, Komorebi urged her friend on, asking folk to make way, or striking their shins with her staff if her commands fell upon deaf ears.

Eventually, the two finalists reached a clearing in the crowd. At its centre stood a pair of majestic trees. They were the walnut trees the two women had passed by on the first day. Now their boles and branches were decorated in ribbons, one all in red, the other in silver. Between their broad spreading roots hung two gonfalons, each hurriedly embroidered with the names of the two finalists.

As the two contestants climbed up the short slope of the berm and appeared above the heads of the crowd, a great cheer rippled through the valley. A mixed flock of small birds erupted from the upper branches of the walnut trees, swirling in confusion before heading west towards the slowly sinking sun. Defeated competitors created a quadrangle on the grassy stage, and as one, bent down on one knee and offered their axes as a mark of respect. Enthusiastic applause, chanting of the finalist's names, and an over-eager horn blower conspired to drown out a celebratory speech attempted by a portly dignitary. Another man stepped forward offering his velvet hat to pick a random token. Codrina recognised him as the one who had registered her name. Her rival suggested Codrina should make the pick, and as she put her hand forward Souchen gave her a little wink and whispered her good fortune. Codrina revealed a silver token and she immediately looked to her chosen walnut tree, reading its bark, form, and stature as though it were a book.

A hush of anticipation descended across the valley as man and woman walked the short distance towards their allotted trees. The finalists stood poised beside their trees, axes in hands, waiting for a signal to begin. A child cried, a horse whinnied, and the faint breeze stirred the ribbons in Codrina's tree.

Further down the valley, a rushing stroked the naked trees, then the ground began to tremble. A single scream, a woman's primeval cry, carried through the silence. Shouts of alarm began to erupt from the perimeter of the crowd.

Codrina whirled round, trying to pinpoint the sources of alarm, but within a few moments she was surrounded by a riot of noise. The ground shook violently and the crowd began to stampede, rushing in all directions as terrible screams began to fill the air. Beyond the gay ribbons and festive colours of the crowds, a dark horde appeared, massed shoulder to shoulder, rushing inward. Even from a distance it was obvious that innocent people were being mown down like wheat before a scythe. Within the blur of slashing weapons and a violent red mist, hands were raised ineffectually to protect or submit. Bodies fell and were trampled, screams silenced abruptly. Ripples of terror became a tsunami of panic.

From her commanding position next to the walnut tree, Codrina watched the horrors unfurl as her mind began to slow. Her thoughts drifted in a dream, observing bodies gripped by terror and violence, swords thrusting, poleaxes swinging, lips grimacing. Her world became silent.

Now there were few of the crowd remaining in front of her. Their numbers briefly swelled as Souchen left her side, leading a charge with many of the braver competitors. With timber axes raised they rushed forward, only to be disappear as though diving into a lake of gall ink. Then the hideous horde filled her vision, halting en bloc in a crescent before her, their monochrome filth obliterating all signs of life. Sound returned to her in a rush of growls, yelps, and snarls.

From the back of the horde, a co-ordinated movement

of poleaxes, swords, and halberds tilted as the mass of dark hoods cleft apart, as if the Earth itself was opening a void. A single dark figure moved through them towards Codrina. She felt every hair rise on her body and instinctively tightened her grip on the walnut shaft of her axe.

In a sudden blur, a green-clad figure rushed from her side, heading straight towards the darkness; fearless and determined. 'No!' Codrina shouted, although she was unsure if the command even left her lips. If it did, it had no effect as Komorebi continued to hurtle headlong towards the centre of the crescent. As her own legs sprang into action, there was a movement in Codrina's peripheral vision, momentarily distracting her. The jaws of a giant wolf, already dripping bright with blood, was tearing through the dark massed ranks. The doomserfs began to scatter under his belly as he towered above them, but none escaped the stamp, slash, and bite of Raunsveig as he tore through them.

Codrina found herself moving, rushing down the small slope towards the tall leader who was now surrounded by a defensive orb of frantic doomserfs. Nearby, Komorebi was among the dark mass, flashes of green lighting her progress towards the same target.

A shadow suddenly covered the valley, only moments before two bolts of darkening came in quick succession. The ground shook terribly and for a long moment the blackness was so absolute, none of the battlefield was visible. The thunderclaps drowned all sound. It was as if life on Earth has been snuffed out.

Codrina's senses returned and now she could see the

leader, edging closer. His arm had been aloft as he beckoned his forces. She watched him lower it and move forward, gaining speed. Codrina knew this was her moment and rushed onward, closing the distance quickly. Only the main orb of doomserfs remained together, while around them hundreds of others were in disarray, pursued by the snarling and chomping wolf. Codrina scanned the emptying valley for Komorebi but could no longer see her, nor the glow of her life-force among the fleeing hordes, yet she had no time to search for her friend.

At last, in front of her now, stood the final few; dark and drooling.

En mass, they abruptly halted as a new terror entered their spirits. Their bodies began to glow as light seemingly filled them from within. A dazzling green began to shine from their eyes and mouths, bursting from oozing wounds, exploding from limb and muscle. Sharp shadows appeared on the ground and among their ranks. Weapons dropped as arms tried to shield eyes from the blinding light.

Codrina lowered her hand, allowing the doomserfs to fall to the ground, like the long shadow of a mountain is erased by the rising sun.

Now she could focus her attention on the lone figure of Xuan. Their leader stood unmoving, surrounded by his decimated hordes, as if their demise was of no consequence. His gaze met hers and a grin tugged at his grey lips.

She focussed her beam once more, but an equal force resisted. Darkness and lightful elements swirled in frantic combat in the space between them. Then Xuan took a step forward, forcing the boundary between life and death back towards the girl. Codrina stood her ground.

A soaring raven high in the sky over Xuan's shoulder appeared frozen mid-soar, a croak caught between its bearded throat and heavy beak. A dribble of bright blood hung weightless below Xuan's sword tip, glinting like a twisted red icicle. Under the sole of his hovering boot, a beautiful pink flower of meadow saxirose had ceased trembling, its face turned towards a motionless bumblebee, heavy with yellow pollen sacs. Droplets of dew hung poised among the tall heads of Cat-tail and a tiny whorled snail paused under a curved blade of grass, one of its antennae partly withdrawn. Then the wind stirred.

Cosmic clouds spiralled between the two figures, arcs of brilliant green shining and flashing in a haze within a black miasma, bolts of darkening striking, absorbing, obliterating.

Suddenly, among the chaotic vapours, a dazzling splinter of green pierced its way through the chaos towards the figure of Xuan. At its sharp end, something flickered in the light, spinning and tumbling along the path of the light.

Codrina's spinning axe flew as true as only vengeance deserves.

The croak of the raven reached Codrina's ears as her axe blade struck Xuan on the forehead. It hit with such force, he was rend asunder. Xuan's hideous face split wide open, revealing a darkness deeper than any void. What remained of his mouth gasped open and air rushed outwards, dank and fetid, before reversing with enough power to disturb and lift the ashes from nearby bodies of his former horde. Wisps of grey and black rushed into his form as it fell to the ground, his body shaking and trembling. It lay there, twitching, yet prostrate.

His conqueror's green cloak billowed towards him as Codrina took her final steps to reach the teratoidal terror lying on the ground before her. Codrina's fingers felt slowly for the familiar antler handle tucked into her belt. She bent over and calmly pushed the blade of her knife slowly and deliberately through the dark mass where a heart might be. The radiant faces of her mother and father flashed in her mind. Streams of molten black lava began to ooze from Xuan's wounds, burning and blackening the earth round the deathless form of embodied evil, once known, and feared by all.

Far, far away, and high in the tower of the Cenobium, Mother Elder looked up from her scriptures, and wondered at the birds rising from the cliffs in such numbers they obliterated the setting sun. Their cries drowned out the pounding of the White Sea's waves far below, and for the briefest moment it seemed as if the Earth herself skipped a heartbeat. Then she understood. She allowed her lonely heart to warm and a lightful smile to grace her lips.

59

Karişkir had split from her band of travellers soon after reaching the Great Forest of Askraland. It wasn't long after continuing to follow the trail of Codrina and Komorebi beyond Bosquillas del Argintas, that Karişkir started to hear unbelievable tales from tinkers and travellers. As the number of stories grew, and details from one or another began to confirm the truth or dismiss the fanciful, her heart filled with dread and hope in equal measure.

She hurried against the trickle of worried souls, which soon became a steady flow of the troubled. Karişkir knew she drew close when she was forced to weave between lines of horrifically injured people. Man, woman, and child appeared to be indiscriminately maimed, the severity of wounds worsening as she neared the origin of the event. Finally, from a tree-clad ridge she gazed in horror at the scene of a huge battlefield spread out before her. Palls of grey smoke drifted across the blackened valley. Few shattered and splintered forms rose above a low mist gathering around the river, among them two large trees growing on a small berm drew her eye.

The bodies were too numerous, to dense upon the ground, to avoid stepping onto and into, accompanied by sickening crunches and explosions of ash. Her shoes and pantaloons were black, and the bottom of her cloak no longer green, by the time she reached the centre of the battlefield. The stench of death and burning cloyed her throat. When she came upon the berm, Karişkir noticed the trees were a pair of majestic walnuts, their branches festooned with tattered ribbons of red and silver. Their roots flowed like water over the small, rounded hill, in places worn smooth from centuries of trampling, in others exposed by recent events, torn and open, bleeding into the grass. Her eye caught sight of a walnut lying where the roots of the two trees appeared to meet. Instinctively, Karişkir knew it would never prosper under their combined canopies and pocketed the large round seed.

From the vantage of the berm, she spied a clearing of bright green grass among the ankle-deep ash. She made her way tentatively towards it, stepping between bodies where she could. It looked very similar to the scene she'd come across in the mountains, except here, at its centre, life had not been preserved. Instead, the crisp black shadow of a body was clearly visible upon the ground. Karişkir knelt and pressed her palm onto its shape and a shiver coursed through her.

Everything she saw with her own eyes, every reek and stench, every crunch of bones, confirmed the stories of eyewitnesses. An army had appeared from among the trees and attacked the innocent crowds at the silvan tournament. No one knew where they had originated, nor their purpose, except to wreak havoc and bring death to the region. It was told that there were two women in green who took the fight to the attackers. One had killed thousands by her own hand before succumbing to some kind of weapon brought down from the sky. Some spoke of a giant bloodthirsty wolf which aided the women, evidently to be dismissed as fancy. As for the other woman in green, some say she disappeared among a brilliant flash, others were adamant that she had remained on the battlefield long enough to build a memorial to her compatriot. Many were convinced the woman was little more than a girl—in fact very like herself, now that she asked—and the same whose name had been on everyone's lips the day before. The woman was named Codrina, and she was due to be crowned champion woodsman of all Askraland. The first time in history that the honour would fall to a woman.

Karişkir's shoulders trembled as she buried her face in blackened hands and her tears flowed unchecked. Not only by the likelihood that Komorebi had lost her life, but also because the trail had gone cold. Where should she turn now? She couldn't return to the Cenobium with ifs and maybes, and in any case, she had come all this way for one reason, and one reason alone. She wondered if she might head towards Bruachavn, passing through the main body of The Great Forest. Given its famed size, there was little hope she would find any further clues about Codrina's whereabouts, or even if she might still be alive. The sounds of her distress suddenly cut through her misery. She was unaware she had been howling, crying like a wolf in the night.

60

The coppices were over-stood, whilst under the taller trees the forest floor lay dark and lifeless. The woods were in desperate need of the deft touch of a forester. As for the garden, it was overrun with weeds and clogged by dense thickets of bramble except where lapinettes had made their burrows. Here and there, birches had taken root and were already well above the height of most men.

The woman took a few more tentative steps forward. As her legs brushed through the knee-high dewy grass, her foot struck something solid hidden among the roots and dead leaves. Pausing to listen again and satisfied to hear the sounds of nature waking and nothing else, she stooped down to inspect the object.

The woman gasped and stifled a little cry. She had picked up a child's doll, beautifully hand-carved from a single piece of ashenwood. Its painted features were faded and if it once wore any clothes—which she knew it did— the little forester was naked except for a little wooden axe fixed to one hand. She clasped it to her chest, sobbing. With her free hand Codrina wiped tears from her cheeks.

As she slowly approached the door to her family home, Codrina was finally certain that no one was living in the house, even though the garden told her the same. It was a relief to see the wooden roof tiles still intact, while none of the panes were broken. If it were not for a wild untamed honeysuckle rampaging over the doorway, she could almost have believed that her parents were still inside, and she was returning to greet them. Her heart lurched as she wrestled the twisted woody stems to the side and pressed down on the door latch.

The door swung open in her hand with a soft creak. A broken stem of ivy caught under the door, brushing an arc through a thick layer of dust lying on the stone flags. Instantly, the scent of the place carried Codrina back through time. She thought for a moment the room had been rearranged, before realising her view of the kitchen was from a new heady height. Codrina treaded lightly, as though walking upon hallowed ground, her feet taking her unbidden to the table at the centre of the room. Under them she knew lay the essence of her parents, and sure enough as she bent down and ran her fingertips through the dust, the dark stains of their flesh and blood were still visible.

Bright sunshine suddenly broke through the dirty windowpane, its low rays streaming through the dust laden air. It wouldn't take too long to clean the place and make it habitable once again. The garden and woods were another matter entirely. Codrina stood and made her way into the narrow scullery. There on a low peg hung her father's forester jacket. She ran her fingers down its dense woollen weave, dipping her hand into the pocket where once her tiny hand had discovered the knife which came to play a major part in her life. Expecting to find it empty, she was surprising to find several hard and cool items lying at the bottom of the pocket. They clinked together as she gathered them together in her fingers and withdrew her hand.

Codrina could not believe her eyes. She recognised every one of the beautiful silver rings which once adorned her spirit mother; the woman who had saved her life countless times. She gazed in wonder at Komorebi's gift, her thoughts drowning in grief. The only explanation must be that she found Codrina's home at some point in her travels and left the rings for her to discover. Such generosity and intelligent foresight epitomised her friend. Tears welled again.

A moving shadow fell briefly across the room and passed over her. Someone had passed across the window outside.

Hurriedly, Codrina shoved the rings into her pockets, reached for the axe on her back, and poised herself on the balls of her feet. She was ready to defend or to attack, brimming with fearsome anger. A figure appeared in the doorway, its silhouette disguised by a cloak and hood.

'Codrina, are you there?' cried out a familiar spirited voice.

The sight of the female warrior rushing from the shadows, her axe poised as if to strike, scared Karişkir more than she would ever admit in all their years together. Yet moments later, as the two friends embraced, kissed, and embraced again, her heart hammered in her chest more from love than fear.

'How did you find me?' asked Codrina, reaching out to touch a loose flame of Karişkir's hair.

'It wasn't easy, especially after the battlefield when your trail went cold.'

'So, how did you? I've been so careful to ...'

Codrina and Karişkir embraced again, this time more closely in silent wonder at the energy which flowed between them. Their eyes locked and they kissed again, this time passionately, even though Codrina still clasped her axe in her hand.

A scratching started on the door, and it slowly creaked open, allowing birdsong and a sweet spring breeze to drift into the tiny cottage. Soft footsteps padded across the stone flags. Codrina cried for joy, dropping her axe onto the kitchen table as she ran to meet the true form of her spirit friend. She wrapped her arms around Raunsveig and buried her face in the warm neck of the timber wolf.

In the beginning, came light and dark.
Where there was, became lightful;
Where there was not, became darkness.

In the light grew life;
Among life, the living made love,
And love bore power over darkness.
Where love failed, darkness prospered,
Bearing hate, malice, and death.

Those that hold the light shall have power over darkness,
And from their wombs bear seeds of love.
Those that crave the dark shall fear lightness,
And their voids devour love.

Those whom carry light in their soul,
Those whom move against the darkness,
Those for whom self is other, and other is life,
They are the lightful, and they shall walk among us.

Together they shall teach the light, and carry the light.
Until the day of parousia comes,
When there shall be born from the heart of trees,
A child to conquer evil.

She shall generate in her soul the beam of life,
And grow to overcome the darkness.
Her given name and being shall be of the forest,
Her name shall be Codrina.

ROOTS, I:I-6

EPILOGUE

WUKA

MASTER THE FORCES OF LIFE

The true rules of Wuka are lost in time, and while many have imagined them, the true nature of the game remains a mystery. It is likely that the game of cards and coins was played by five players. What is known is that the game centred on the five elements of life on Earth: wood, fire, earth, metal, and water. These were related to one another and interdependent, governed only by naturalness, spontaneity, and chaos. All elements were created equal but had different powers in the hands of five different player characters who attempted to be their masters: Forester, Stoker, Miner, Smith, and Sailor. Each character had subtly different powers. Elements and characters were influenced by four different forces, some good and others bad by differing degrees: generating, overcoming, deficient, and excessive. The power of forces flowing between elements was determined by characters at any moment in time. The first player to secure control over all five natural elements was triumphant. It is evident players had to yield their powers with cunning subtlety while navigating the random forces of nature to yield an ultimate mastery of life.

Generating forces
* Wood feeds fire
* Fire creates earth (ash)
* Earth bears metal
* Metal collects water
* Water nourishes wood

Overcoming forces
* Wood parts earth
* Earth absorbs water
* Water quenches fire
* Fire melts metal
* Metal chops wood

Deficient forces
* Wood dulls Metal
* Metal de-energises Fire
* Fire evaporates Water
* Water destabilises Earth
* Earth rots Wood

Excessive forces
* Wood depletes Earth
* Earth obstructs Water
* Water extinguishes Fire
* Fire vaporises Metal
* Metal over-harvests Wood

EPIC POEM

THE LEGEND OF PAROUSIA

What! A tale of a time || From troubadours of yore
When working woods || Were wooed in whispers
In tongues a tenon deep || Sung in respectful timbre
By a wisdom woven in nature || Nurturing a home of wild
While bavins baked || And ships sailed on bended knee
The woodsman wielded his axe || Breathing life to the world
Yet as sun and moon sauntered || Ignorant in celestial solitude
Unbeknown a fracture formed || And beneath it, a foulness
A shadow of shade || A darkness in the shallows
Its cryptic camouflage || Found the nightjar kipping
Unseen by tawny owl to tell || Or even tiny pipistrelle
By lurking under root and limb || Girding its fearsome loins
Preparing an evil power || Making its vile plans
Came the one whose name we quietly swear || That diavol Xuan

Now ready to unleash an underworld || Except for the underling
Forged in the forest || That silvan fay
Who might cultivate a mighty crown || Unless her bud is cut
So, in a storm of his design || Her procreators are cruelly slain
Yet his pursuit is parried || And a magical riposte
Carried in a flying kernel || To strike upon and kill
And one doomserf dragged away || By a rival devilry
An impenetrable puzzle || Unexpected among leaf and petiole
Leaving his fury to fester || For his quarry has now fled
He senses her in the city || And still she escapes
First a crushing fire || Then a frenzied firestorm
And all the while he wonders || Who and why
The green woman waits || Determined to watch over
The girl who he finds has grown || Into a gallant boy
Lured and lingering ready to die || Again she lives and leaves
Then distracted by a mortal man || In a final act of mettle
Once again our seed is saved || Her spirit free
To sail across the sea || In search of answers
In her possession a powerful axe || Forged with passion
Its blade born of walnut || A soul for the brave
Its haft deftly hewn || From a walnut heart
And born from a silver band || On its deathly blade
A fierce-some face || Of one we no longer fear
With golden gaze || And fur of grey
Raunsveig, the wolf of reverie || the wolf of renascence
But then! Our seedling suffers again || Cruelly shipwrecked
By a White Sea storm || Or a dark sea serpent
Only to survive and stay afloat || In a wooden nest encircled
And finally born to a foreign shore || Whereupon she is found
As a wounded woman || To be taken under the wing
Of the celebrated Cenobites || Her fate now sealed
And so! The legend was learned || In the cloistered library

As the oracler laid out her origins || And her future to come
Generating and overcoming || A force in the making
Wood to part earth || Earth to Absorb Water
Water to quench fire || Fire to melt metal
Metal to chop wood || Wood to feed the earth
The nature of nurture || A life for every creature
Where darkness will be diminished || The diavol dismissed
At last! Our divine deity || Our Codrina is finally delivered
To begin her quest || Driven from deep within her breast
An epic effort || To evict evil
Underground || And overground
In mountain snow || And desert sun
Then along the route || A reunion ruined
By a thunderous bolt || From a darkening body
Dispelled by a brilliant green || In a focussed beam
Our heroine discovers || Her power within
Now a battle won || But a war yet to win
Somewhere and sooner || Than Codrina suspects
For the hordes now massing || In horrid ranks
Among the green growth || Of a forest grove
Dark and dangerous || Beckoning death
A silvan celebration || To welcome spring
Lures the darkness || Beckons the devil
So, in a sickle crescent || They scythe the crowds
Doomserfs swarming || Celebrants dying
Until with jaws to rip and roar || Comes Raunsveig
Scattering below his belly of fur || They begin to flee
Even as the beam is borne || By a Cenobite
A spirit mother || A sacrifice made
In love and living || With conquering light
Before two darkening bolts || Are brought to bear
Then our warrior is ready || And with fist raised

Shines so brilliantly || None can stand
Except darkness himself || In deathly defence
Their forces fighting || Light and dark flashing
The beam balanced || Its power blocked
But then, as foretold || Our fearsome female
Lets fly her weapon || Forged in wonder
To spin unstoppable || And cleave and split
The diavol's head divided || Revealing the void of death
His fluids to spill and flow || Back to the world below
Oh miracle, now forged! || From a sister forester
The green gold of life || A light shone, a warmth granted
Banishing sorrow and shadow || Forging joy and solace
And so! My story is told || Now you too can tell the tale
Of the epic escapade || The caper and crusade
The query and quest || Of a conquering trio
The Wolf, the Walnut || And the Woodsman.

Retrieved from the remains of the Library of Cenobium,
Leybosque in the year of Our Lady 3041

BOOKS BY GABRIEL HEMERY

FICTION
Green Gold
Tall Trees Short Stories: Volume 20
Tall Trees Short Stories: Volume 21

Also Featured in:
Arboreal
Stories of Trees, Woods, and the Forest

NON-FICTION
The New Sylva

In Press
The Forest Guide: Scotland

www.gabrielhemery.com/books

ABOUT THE AUTHOR

Dr Gabriel Hemery is an author, tree photographer, and
silvologist (forest scientist). He has written many books,
both fiction and non-fiction, and appears regularly on TV
and radio talking about trees and the environment. He co-
founded Sylva Foundation, an environmental charity, and
is currently its Chief Executive. Gabriel writes a top-
ranking tree blog featuring his books and photography.

www.gabrielhemery.com

ACKNOWLEDGEMENTS

I am indebted to so many wonderful people. To my wife and family for their forbearance of my writing habits and obsession with this story. To my regular readers for their encouragement and support. To my beta-readers, even if they chose to remain anonymous. For help with maps, the community of Wonderdraft. Finally, to J.R. for nurturing inspiration.

CPSIA information can be obtained
at www.ICGtesting.com
Printed in the USA
LVHW092051200522
719225LV00014B/386